RUBE GOLDBERG

AND HIS AMAZING MACHINES

⚙ THE NEW SWITCHEROO ⚙

THE NEW SWITCHEROO

By Brandon T. Snider

In collaboration with Jennifer George
and the Estate of Rube Goldberg

Illustrated by Ed Steckley

AMULET BOOKS • NEW YORK

Cataloging-in-Publication Data has been applied for and may be obtained from the Library of Congress.

ISBN 978-1-4197-5006-9

Text © 2022 Heirs of Rube Goldberg
Illustrations by Ed Steckley
Book design by Brenda E. Angelilli and Chelsea Hunter

Printed and bound in U.S.A.
10 9 8 7 6 5 4 3 2 1

Amulet Books are available at special discounts when purchased in quantity for premiums and promotions as well as fundraising or educational use. Special editions can also be created to specification. For details, contact specialsales@abramsbooks.com or the address below.

Amulet Books® is a registered trademark of Harry N. Abrams, Inc.

ABRAMS The Art of Books
195 Broadway, New York, NY 10007
abramsbooks.com

For Travis

RUBE GOLDBERG

AND HIS AMAZING MACHINES

✿ THE NEW SWITCHEROO ✿

CHAPTER 1

"Where is Rube Goldberg?!"

Pearl was at her wit's end. For weeks she'd worked tirelessly alongside her classmates to revamp Beechwood Middle School's dilapidated old garden. They gathered every morning, shovels in hand, and dug up that sad patch of dirt like their lives depended on it. Their mission wasn't just about beautification. It was about building something they could be proud of. It was about planting seeds and watching the chain reaction of nature's life cycle turn them into a bountiful harvest come the start of fall. Pearl and her friends had helped turn the garden into something very special and they'd done it by working together. It was a source of pride for everyone involved. Especially considering how neglected the garden looked before they got started. Some plants were wilted, others devoured by ravenous groundhogs. The dirt was dry, and the adjoining pond had grown mossy and brown. No frogs. No fish. No life at all. It broke Pearl's heart. But what really steamed her buns on this airy Saturday morning was something else entirely.

"I'm going to kill that kid . . ." When Pearl told Rube about her plan to refurbish the garden, she hoped he'd help out. Till the soil. Maybe rake a little. But that wasn't how Rube's brain worked. When he looked at that dusty patch of land, all he saw were problems that needed solving. *Which is a good thing.* First and foremost, how would the garden stay hydrated? With fall creeping in and a dry winter right behind it, how could vegetables and plants possibly be expected to grow without a little help? For days Rube burned the midnight oil thinking about this conundrum. Then, after a raindrop splashed his nose on a bright sunny day, the answer came to him. *I'll build a self-watering garden system!* He had quickly sketched a design, then scrounged around town for machine parts. After he selected only the finest pieces, a masterpiece was surely forthcoming. But, in true Rube fashion, his simple idea had become lot more complex. *And stressful.*

"This is *so* typical of Goldberg. *So typical,*" Pearl grumbled, pacing back and forth as she cracked her knuckles. "I should have seen this coming."

Pearl had been beyond excited after Rube signed on to help, and not just because they were close friends. His star had risen considerably in recent weeks. The whole school was talking about

Rube's amazing machine-making skills ever since he had unknowingly taken down an international criminal who just happened to be masquerading as one of their science teachers. *More on that later.* The students at Beechwood Middle School couldn't wait to see his next big creation, and all eyes were on the garden project. If Pearl pulled this off, that meant good things for the school *and* her campaign to become sixth-grade class president. *A double whammy.*

Once Rube got wind of all that bubbling anticipation, the more pressure he felt. The more pressure he felt, the more stressed out he became. *What if I can't top myself? What if everyone thinks my success is a fluke? What if I've lost my mojo? WHAT IS MOJO ANYWAY?!* It felt cool to have the admiration of his classmates, but one wrong move and those bloodthirsty vultures would eat him alive. At least that was what he told himself. The imagined pressure had driven Rube to drop the ball completely.

Work stopped just as quickly as it started, and he moved on to something else. The problem was, he hadn't told Pearl he'd given up. Quite the opposite. Pearl was under the impression Rube was busy building an exquisite monument to nature itself. *The future of horticulture!* Nothing was further from the truth. In a bid to cover his blunder, he decided to double down on the ruse. The night before the big reveal, using a handful of billowing blue tarps, Rube had erected a small tent around the garden and adjoining pond. A crude sign warned people DO NOT TOUCH. He hadn't wanted anyone knowing his shameful secret. Not even Pearl. It was a terrible plan, but that was what he had done. Now, on the day of the garden's grand unveiling, Pearl faced a crowd of classmates, teachers, and local press. She had no idea what to do next. Rube Goldberg was nowhere to be found.

"If he's not here in five minutes, I'm going to . . . to . . ." Pearl struggled to come up with a suitable punishment, but words failed her. "I don't know!"

Rube's best friend, Boob, peeked around the edge of the tent to spy on the growing crowd. "Wow. It's like a who's who of middle school royalty showed up for this thing! I see Emilia Harris, Aiden Puterbaugh-Schmidt, and that kid who smells like lunch meat who we call Ham Pockets."

"But where's Rube?!" exclaimed Pearl. "I called him. I texted him. What am I supposed to do if he doesn't show up?! He's the only one who knows how to operate whatever contraption is under that tarp. Public embarrassment is not on my to-do list for today."

Boob thought about it for a second. "Maybe he's been abducted by aliens? Though honestly, if *I* were an alien, he wouldn't be my first choice. Love the guy. Obvi. But the kid is *a lot* to handle."

He spotted a few more familiar faces as the congregation grew larger. "*Ugh.* Someone let Mike and Ike out of their cages. Why did those dungballs come *here*? Oh, oh, oh! Davin Drake is in attendance, looking fly as usual. Wow. The guy's smile can sure light up a room."

Pearl felt the same, but there were far more important things on her mind. "I *need* this to go smoothly today. We put a lot of hard work into making this garden sparkle. And, yeah, we don't have crops yet, but next year we will! We'll have a beautiful, botanical wonderland filled with delights! Those people out there are here to celebrate that. They came to see the machine demonstration, and . . ." She trailed off. "Rube is a no-show."

Suddenly an idea popped into Boob's head. "I bet I can find him with my Li'l Sleuthy Kid Detective Kit. My mom got it for me for my birthday even though I stopped watching *Li'l Sleuthy*, like, a million years ago. I mean . . . *a baby detective*?! And his sidekick is *a talking magnifying glass*?! Total kids' stuff."

"Boob . . ." Pearl's words were slow and purposeful. "I know you're only trying to help, but please stop talking now."

Boob nodded. "Copy that."

"Heyo!" Principal Kim exclaimed, popping behind the tent for a quick check-in. "How's everything going, Pearl? The crowd is getting antsy. You ready to start?"

"Yep!" Pearl straightened up, put on a happy face, and pretended everything was just fine. Principal Kim had become one of the garden project's biggest supporters. She didn't want to let him down. "I just need *one more minute,* if you don't mind."

"Sounds good! We're all looking forward to your presentation," replied Principal Kim. "Oh, and if you could mention the merchandise for sale on our school website, that would be awesome. I've got a warehouse full of Beechwood Bandicoot caftans that need to move. At twenty dollars each, they're a steal. Free shipping too! Just sayin'."

After Principal Kim exited the area, Pearl grabbed Boob by his shoulders and looked him square in the eyes. "I need you to stall," she said, panicked.

"Me? Really?" Boob began sweating. "You know Ahmed Brooks is sitting in the front row, right? He does magic! He's not *good* at it, but he *does* it. His pockets are always full of sponge balls and handkerchiefs. It's creepy. You should ask *him* to stall. He's way more prepared than I am."

"Boob!" Pearl stopped herself, took a deep breath, and continued in a calmer fashion. "All I need you to do is talk for a few minutes while I come up with a plan to explain away Rube being a no-show. *That's it.* You're good at talking. Some say *too good.*

Please just do this for me so I don't lose my head?"

Boob considered the request. "Well, I *have* thought about pursuing a career in stand-up comedy," he confessed. "My uncle Rodney was a comedian, you know . . ."

"Great! Tell jokes, do impressions, make balloon animals."

"What about hand puppets?"

"*Anything you want*," Pearl growled. "Just do it!" She pushed him out from behind the tent into full view of the crowd. "Make Uncle Rodney proud," she said, beaming.

All eyes were on Boob. Everyone quieted as he confidently strolled to the front of the staging area. As Rube's trusty hype man, Boob was used to hamming it up. He was a natural entertainer whose positive energy was infectious. The kid could make a stone statue crack a smile. But if you put him on the spot? That made him a wee bit nervous.

"So . . . ummmm . . ." Boob audibly gulped, but there was no turning back now. "Did you guys hear the one about the shoemaker who gave away his fortune? Turns out he had a really good *sole*. Hehe." A flurry of tiny giggles vibrated through the crowd, putting Boob's heart at ease. *They liked him.* In an instant, a switch flipped inside Boob, transforming him into comedian boy. "Ladies and gentlemen, I'm Boob McNutt, and yes, that's my real name. What can I say? My parents had great taste! It was either Boob McNutt or Nitwit Macadamia VonCashew McNutt. I think they made the right choice." The giggles turned to guffaws and the jokes came hard and fast.

"Hey, what do you call aliens that eat eggs? Eggs-traterrestrials!

"Are monsters good at math? Of course not!" Boob stuck his finger in the air as if he'd just had a massive revelation. "Unless you *Count Dracula.*

"What do you get when you cross a dinosaur with a firework? Dinomite!

"Why are cigarettes so deadly? Because they travel in packs! That joke made my aunt Linda laugh so hard, it gave her coughing fits. She's also a smoker. Well, *was* a smoker. She passed away from lung cancer last year." The crowd fell awkwardly silent. "Guess you could say it *took her breath away*!" The laughter returned once again. "You guys are *dark*. I'm into it."

"Boooo!" a voice shouted. "You suck, McNutt!" another called out. Mike and Ike, the twin bully blockheads, loved sharing their opinions, even when no one wanted to hear them. Why they were at this particular event was anybody's guess. Boob was unfazed by their jeers.

"Oh look, Beechwood's most famous twins, Mike and Ike, are here! Or, as I like to call them, Copy and Paste. I asked their mom which one was her favorite. Know what she said? *Neither*. One day those two troublemakers will end up in jail—then they'll *really* be *cellmates*."

Stunned by the sudden barrage of burns, Mike and Ike sat quietly in their chairs and grumbled to themselves. Boob was on a roll and the crowd was eating him right up.

"Y'all into astronomy? Have you heard the one about *Uranus*?"

Pearl ran up behind Boob, surprising him. "And thank you, Boob! What a king of comedy! My sides hurt from all the chuckles . . ."

"But I was just getting started. I'm on fire!"

"I'll take it from here, thanks," Pearl whispered.

"But where's Rube?"

Pearl shook her head. "Not here." With time running out, there was no choice but to press forward without him. Boob moved to the side as Pearl took command. "Thank you all so much for coming. My name is Pearl Williams, and I'm a proud officer of the Greenhouse Guild, Beechwood Middle School's premier garden club. Like many of my classmates, I was saddened to find our garden in disarray. But my fellow Guild members and I knew that, with a little love and affection, great things could grow here again!" The crowd went wild, clapping and hollering with glee. "Hope everyone likes kale, spinach, broccoli, Brussels sprouts, cauliflower, kohlrabi, beets, and peas! Next year, when our harvest is good and ready, we'll be selling veggies to anyone who wants them!" Pearl exclaimed, pumping her fist in the air. Sadly, she was met with total silence. The crowd was decidedly unenthused about vegetables.

Except for Ami Sato, the school's most passionate vegetarian. "Woo-hoo!" Ami shouted. "Give it up for beets!" She clapped her hands so hard, they turned bright red. Pearl stood grinning silently until Ami quieted down.

"I'd like to thank my fellow Greenhouse Guild members for their support and commitment, and I'd also like to thank Lala Palooza for her generous donation that made this transformation possible." Pearl motioned to Lala, who was sitting in the back looking like a wealthy old widow, incognito in a pair of dark designer sunglasses. If not for the newly dyed purple streaks in her hair, she would've been easy to miss. "Lala, please come forward so we can—"

"No, thanks. This is *all you*, Pearly girl." Lala stood and gave a half-hearted wave to the assemblage. It was all she felt like doing today. Normally Lala loved being the center of attention but, when it came to matters of charity, she preferred to avoid the spotlight. *Give the money and run.*

Pearl cleared her throat and continued addressing the crowd. "We are so lucky to have a self-watering garden system built by none other than Rube Goldberg! Who is with us in spirit." The crowd gasped in shock. "But not dead! He's very much alive." The crowd breathed a sigh of relief. "At least until I get my hands on him," Pearl said under her breath. Her palms were drenched with sweat. "What else . . . what else . . . ? Oh! Please check out the Beechwood Middle School website, where you can find an exciting selection of gifts for Bandicoots of all ages." Principal Kim waved his arms to get Pearl's attention, mouthing the word *caftan* over and over again. "And caftans!" she said joyfully. "Does everyone know the Beechwood Bandicoot fight song? Let's sing it now!" Even a handful of scattered groans couldn't stop her from continuing the time-wasting charade. "We are the Bandicoots, the mighty Beechwood Bandicoots . . ."

As the song dragged on, Pearl gazed out into the distance. She hoped to see Rube speeding toward her on his bike, ready to swoop in and save the day. He'd pull up, apologize for his tardiness, then dazzle everyone with his machine-making talents. The crowd would eat it up, and Pearl's first organized event would be deemed a wild success. But it had become painfully clear that wasn't happening, and as the song came to a close, she was forced to accept the reality of the situation.

"Show us the garden already!" a voice shouted.

The jig was up. There was no more time to waste. The moment of truth had arrived. Pearl grasped the edge of the tarp. "Here goes nothing . . ." she said, whipping it off the tent and revealing the beautifully reimagined garden. It was an exquisite sight to behold. Vibrantly colored signs, hand painted by art students, adorned each area where herb and vegetable seeds had been planted. A newly constructed trellis stood tall and proud. The once-murky pond had been transformed into a self-watering system, which was primed and ready to go.

Thankfully, Pearl wouldn't have to try and operate it by herself, because under that tent was a delightful, off-putting surprise. Rube Goldberg was napping peacefully, cuddled up with his machine like it was his blankie. The day was saved. Or so Pearl thought. "Rube!" she exclaimed.

The sleepy boy jolted awake. *Oh god. Oh god. Oh god.* As Rube squinted and adjusted his glasses, he grew petrified by the mass of eyes staring him down. "Oh. Hey. Guess I must have conked out," he said, wiping away a bit of spittle. He had laid his head down on his history book, hoping to get a couple minutes of shut-eye before everyone arrived. *Ugh, such a boring book. Put me right to sleep.* He had rolled off it during his nap, ending up face-down in the dirt. The crowd chuckled as he cleaned the crusted soil from his cheek. *They must think this is all part of the show.* Pearl leaned close to Rube so only he could hear her.

"I was worried—"

"Awww. About little ol' me? That's sweet."

"*Let me finish*," Pearl pressed. "I *was* worried. Then I was *mad*. Now I don't know what I am, but that doesn't matter. What I need *you* to do is get up, brush yourself off, and *razzle-freaking-dazzle*."

"You didn't *really* think I'd leave you hanging? Psshhhh. Have faith, girl!"

The night before the event, unbeknownst to anyone, a pit of guilt had begun growing in Rube's stomach after he had deceptively assembled the garden tent. He'd become overwhelmed with

shame for breaking his promise. *What's wrong with me?! Pearl is one of my closest friends on the entire planet. Messing up her big day would make me the Duke of Jerks!* So, Rube had pulled one of his quasi-all-nighters. He had stayed up late, then woken up early to make sure the machine was ready in time. The process had left him exhausted, but he was used to that kind of thing. After a final round of tinkering, Rube had begun yawning like crazy as the sun came up. Overwhelmed by the need for shut-eye, he had found a comfortable place in the dirt and curled up. Next thing he knew, the whole world was watching. *Give or take a few billion people.*

"Don't sweat it. I've got this." Rube leapt from the ground in a burst of energy. "How's everyone doing? Ready to see the Irrigator in action?"

"YEAH!!!" The crowd cheered with renewed vigor. Students hooted and hollered like they were at a championship football game. Their hero had risen from the grime to bestow upon them yet another monument to innovation! Pearl still wanted to wring Rube's neck, but instead she just smiled. The moment was bigger than her feelings. At least that's what she told herself.

"Let's get this baby going . . ." Rube calmly hooked a hose up to a pump and turned a nozzle. A cascade of liquid glory was just around the corner! But nothing happened. Not even a dribble. Now everyone was anxious. "Hrrmm," Rube said, biting his lip. "The solar panels are charged, and the pump from the pond should be working."

Pearl looked out at the crowd and shrugged. "Even geniuses make mistakes, I guess."

Boob moved close to Rube and mumbled in his ear, "Did you catch any of my act? Pretty good, right? I was thinking of auditioning for the town talent show, the Beechwood Follies. Wanna be my helper monkey?"

"Back up, please. I'm trying to work," Rube said, shooing Boob away. *Now is not the time for funny business.* "Aha. I see the problem." Rube fiddled and futzed with the Irrigator, hooking and unhooking hoses, until one of them progressively began to feel thicker. *That's good, right? Wait. Maybe not. Uh-oh.*

FSSSSSSSSSSSS! In an instant, a burst of wild water cascaded across the crowd like a sprinkler. Then *another* burst. *And another.* The rowdy hose swung through the air like a snake, spitting pond water in every direction. In a matter of seconds, the entire crowd was drenched from head to toe. They were shocked, speechless, and soggy.

"Ta-daaaaaa!" Boob exclaimed. He'd escaped the liquid assault and was now posing around Rube's machine like a model from *The Price Is Right.*

Principal Kim pointed at his assistant, Miss Mary, who took off like a shot to parts unknown. The crowd was irritated and so was Pearl. Some people stormed off in a huff while others sat patiently, unsure of what to do next. A handful of upperclassmen cackled wildly, admiring the prank-y-ness of it all. But Pearl wasn't laughing. Not one bit.

"I'm so sorry, everyone," she said softly. "This wasn't supposed to happen."

Miss Mary returned, scrambling to pass out towels she'd grabbed from the nearest locker room inside the school. Though the towels *looked* clean, their odor told a different story. As the crowd dispersed, Rube kept tinkering with the Irrigator. He was determined to find its flaw. *Grrrrr. I checked this thing a million times. Okay, maybe not that many. But I checked it a lot! Ugh. Pearl must*

hate me right now. He reached into the back of his pants, pulled out his notebook, and began double-checking his work. *This goes in there. That goes in there. Huh. Now that I think about it, maybe I should have . . .*

Pearl stood over him, arms folded, glaring. "Do you even understand how embarrassing this was?! If you doomed my chance to become sixth-grade class president, I'm going to haunt you for the rest on your life, Rube."

Before Rube could respond, Lala interrupted. "Oh no, sweetie," she cooed, twirling her freshly dampened locks. "That was *exactly* what your campaign needed. Do I feel disgusting right now? *Yes.* Am I sending you the dry-cleaning bill for my outfit? *Without a doubt.* But that whole scene was kind of *amaze.* You want people to notice you, right?"

"Well, yeah, but . . ."

"Then be happy! All press is good press. *Everyone* will be talking about this. *Trust.*" Lala shuddered with excitement. "Oh, how I live for drama! *Great* reveal with Rube under the tent. I could *really* feel the tension and suspense. And Pearl, the look on your face was priceless. *Puh-rice-less.* You better hope someone recorded a video."

"*Gross*, Lala. I'm not trying to go viral. I don't want this moment out there for everyone to see, even if it does get me noticed.

I want to win the election on merit, not *likes* or *views* or whatever."

"Suit yourself," Lala purred. "But, you know, the Switcheroo Dance is the weekend right before the election. Prime time to do something memorable that'll put you on a path to victory. But I get it. You want to keep things low-key. I can respect that. But if you change your mind and want to cause a scene, let me know. I'm happy to use my social media to further the cause."

Rube's ears perked up. He'd forgotten that the Switcheroo Dance was coming up soon. It was a rite of passage for Beechwood Middle School students. Their first official social engagement of the year. Traditionally, the girls were supposed to ask the boys, hence the "swticheroo." While some kids thought the concept was cute and fun, most kids thought it was lame and outdated. But that never stopped them from going. Rube tried not to think about it. *Stupid old dance, stupid old tradition. You couldn't pay me to go to that thing. Unless . . .*

"Causing a scene isn't really my style, Lala," said Pearl. "I'm going to stick to proving myself as the best candidate by sharing my vision for this school."

"That's the spirit," Principal Kim exclaimed as he dried behind his ears. "Integrity first!"

Pearl winced. "I'm really sorry, Principal Kim. Am I suspended? If I am, please don't tell my parents. They'll literally murder me."

"You did *fine*, Pearl. Embarrassing things happen to the best of us. One time I had to give a speech to an auditorium full of people after I unknowingly sat on a melted candy bar. Everyone thought I had *you-know-what* on the seat of my trousers. I can laugh about it *now*, but when it happened, I felt like crawling into a hole and disappearing for the better part of the next century."

"Principal Kim, that was *us*, and it was *last week*," said Boob.

"My point is, *life goes on*. The garden looks beautiful and that's what matters. We have a wonderful, new, environmentally friendly irrigation system courtesy of Mr. Goldberg that, fingers crossed, will be fixed soon. Rest assured, I'll be showing off your hard work to Superintendent Atwater when he visits. I imagine his heart will swell with Bandicoot pride!"

CLICK! CLANK! CLUNK!

After a bit of dabbling, Rube had successfully located the Irrigator's malfunction. "You'll never believe this, but I got my hoses mixed up. Ha! I'm such a dummy sometimes. Shall we fire this bad boy up one more time?"

"That's not needed," advised Principal Kim. "Just set the timer or do whatever you need to do to automate the process. We'll take a photo later for the school paper."

"AHEM!" Lala had been waiting patiently for Principal Kim to notice her.

"Hello, Miss Pallooza," Principal Kim replied. "How *rare* to see you on school grounds these days."

"I know, right?" Lala said with a smirk. Lately, she preferred staying home and completing her school assignments under the dutiful eyes of her tutor as opposed to attending classes. "But I've been around enough to see what's really going on around here. Remember that gigantic donation I graciously gave our school? Are you going to start putting it to use . . . or no? Because so far, the only changes I've seen are this garden renovation and the new teachers' lounge vending machines."

Principal Kim gasped. "How do you know about those? The teacher's lounge is a *secret sanctuary*," he said. "You can't get in without a passcode."

"I have *ways*," Lala said with a smirk.

Principal Kim ignored the revelation. "Moving on, our new district superintendent, Superintendent Atwater, will be visiting soon, and we'll be discussing how to put your generous donation to good use, Lala. We both want to make sure BMS has everything it needs to thrive."

"Boring!" Boob whined. "Sorry, Principal Kim. It's just that my body needs hot dogs and ice cream *very badly*. Can we go now? Everyone is meeting at the Inside Scoop, and if we get there too late, Mike and Ike will have eaten everything."

Lala waved to her driver. "C'mon. We'll take my ride."

Boob raced over to the waiting limo like a puppy dog. Lala followed close behind, leaving Pearl and Rube to stare at each other blankly. Neither knew what to say. *Apologize, Goldberg. You messed up Pearl's big day. You know you did. Just admit it and move on.* Before Rube could open his mouth, Davin Drake surprised Pearl from behind, putting his arms around her and giving her a big, warm hug. "Congrats on the garden, you two. It's *really* beautiful."

Pearl lit up. "Aw, thanks."

Davin was the kind of kid Rube wished he could be. Smart, silly, genuine. He had great skin and a big heart, and he could talk to *anyone*. He listened to people too. The guy was fearless. And kind! Davin had next-level swag. The most precious of all the swags. His smile ignited a flame inside everyone he came into contact with. Whether they liked it or not.

"Thanks for the shower, Rube! Haha." Davin gave Rube a playful bop on the arm. "Your machine is amazing. It's like you needlessly challenge yourself as a way to grow. Innovation through complication. The way your mind works! What a gift." He turned his attention to Pearl. "Let's go skateboarding this week. We could go over to Willie's and look at decks, *or* if you want to just hang out and watch *Ranma ½*, that's cool."

"I'll text you," Pearl said.

"Right on." Davin flung his skateboard onto the pavement, took a running leap onto it, then glided down the street like the Silver Surfer. "Check ya later!"

Rube pursed his lips. "I didn't know you were into anime." His tone was both suspicious and interested. *I thought I was the only one who knew about* Ranma ½. "Or is that something you only do with Davin?"

Pearl sighed. "You don't know everything about me. Just like I don't know everything about *you*. And that's all right. But if you have something you'd like to tell me, I'm all ears."

Apologize, Goldberg. Do it now. Stop stalling.

"C'mon, you two!" Boob yelled dramatically. *"I'm dying!"*

Before Rube had a chance to smooth things over with Pearl, a surprise guest appeared out of nowhere. *Emilia Harris.* "Hey, machine boy!" she chirped in a high-pitched twang. "I've been waiting for you to talk to me."

Uh, okay? Ever since his uptick in popularity, Emilia had been paying quite a bit of attention to Rube. He found it strange. *Last year she pretended not to know my name, and now she won't leave me alone? Something's up with that girl.* Emilia was popular. An "ice queen" to many, she also had a sweet streak. Her fashionable dress and curiously short new haircut made her stand out, but that stuff didn't matter to Rube. Mostly he humored her out of kindness.

"That water prank was *beyond*. I'm such a fan. Not that I get the whole *machine thing,* but it's cool and everyone loves it. So, I do too!" she said with a pointed giggle.

"Oh. Thanks," Rube said. "It wasn't a *prank*, but, um, that's nice to say?"

Emilia glared at Pearl. "Are you two *together?*"

The question caught Pearl completely off guard. Rube couldn't tell if she loved the question or hated it. As far as he knew, they were just friends. *Right?*

Pearl's face scrunched up in a peculiar way. *"Us? Me* and *Rube?"*

Anxiety bubbles percolated throughout Rube's entire being. *I would like to crawl into a hole, cover myself with dirt, and never come out, please.* The more uncomfortable he became, the more his body language shifted. He put his hands on his hips, wiped his sweaty forehead, then dried his damp hand on his shirt. *This is it. This is the end of my life.* He put his hands in his pockets, rocked back and forth, winced, folded his arms, and shrugged. *Don't speak. Say nothing.* "You mean *Pearl* and *me?" What did I just tell you?!*

Emilia nodded.

"No," Rube and Pearl said in unison. They looked at each other

as if they'd just been caught stealing. Neither of them knew what to do next. Then Pearl looked at her watch.

"I gotta go," she said. "My mom will be mad if I'm not home soon. Chores and stuff. You understand. See you *later*, Rube." Pearl grabbed her bike and hightailed it out of there.

Rube suddenly remembered something about Pearl's watch. *That little liar.* He filed the bit of information away for later.

"I'm running for sixth-grade class president too, just so you know. Kind of a last-minute decision," Emilia told Rube. "Can I count on your support?"

Wow. Way to drop a low-key bombshell. The question left Rube stupefied. *I'm voting for Pearl, of course.* But, in the interest of not starting any conflict, the last thing he wanted to do was upset Emilia. The more he thought about it, the stranger it felt that she was putting him on the spot like that. *We're not even friends! We shared a PB&J once in third grade! That's all!*

Out of the corner of his eye, Rube noticed Boob hanging out the window of Lala's limo, making wildly animated gestures to get his attention. Instead of respectfully telling Emilia no and saying a formal goodbye, Rube simply left. He ran over to the limo, hopped inside, and slammed the door behind him. "Hot dogs and ice cream! STAT!" And that was that.

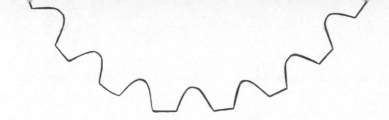

CHAPTER 2

"What was that all about?" Lala crossed her legs and made herself comfortable. "You can't wiggle out of this one, Goldberg. *Spill it.*"

"Emilia was makin' the moves on Rubey-Rube-Rube." Boob wiggled his eyebrows up and down while licking his lips. "I guess she's got a thing for messy-haired inventor boys with dirt on their cheeks and under their nails. *Steeeaaammmyyy.*"

Rube wasn't in the mood. "*First of all*, stop making that face. *Second of all*, we were just talking. And *third of all*, where is there dirt on my cheek?!" He winced at his reflection in the limo's mirrored walls. "Ugh, I look like some ragamuffin who lives under a bridge."

"Emilia Harris has no tact. No grace. She moves through the world like a desperate child. Her social media following is *huge,* but the quality of her content is *shameful.* A circus monkey could come up with better posts." Lala yawned. "All rich girls in this town are positively unbearable. Boring too. Money can't buy you class, I guess."

"Um, Lala, you're rich too. Like, the richest of the rich," Boob reminded her. "Teddy Helden said you use one-dollar bills to wipe your butt. I told him you probably use *five-dollar* bills 'cuz they're *way* classier."

"Stop being disgusting," scolded Rube.

"Sorry," Boob replied. "My bad."

Lala had already stopped paying attention. Her head was in another place entirely. "You don't understand. Having money isn't everything. For instance, my rich parents think vacationing all over

the world and having their photograph taken in exotic locales is more important than spending time with their daughter. A shame, really." Lala cast her eyes downward. Her parents, Javier and Penélope, were rarely in town anymore. Not only had their acting careers taken off, but they'd also become brand ambassadors for a travel website. The job demanded that they zigzag across the world for long periods of time. Not once had they invited Lala along for the ride. *Not once.* It did more than just get on her nerves. It broke her heart. "To paraphrase the French poet Paul Valéry, 'Une personne seule est toujours en mauvaise compagnie.'[1] Well, the way he said it was more gendered. I adapted it for a modern audience."

"Hey!" Boob shouted. "We just passed the Inside Scoop!"

Lala's chauffeur, Hives, piped up from the driver's seat. "We are not going to that dreadful establishment. I'm depositing each of you at your home. Miss Palooza has homework to attend to, and social gatherings are out of the question until she's finished with all of her most pressing assignments."

Boob's eyes widened. *"Do something,"* he whispered to Lala. "I need a big dog with all the fixin's. I was *promised* a big dog with all the fixin's."

Lala poked her face into the front seat. "Hives, I love ya, but we're going for ice cream. Turn this thing around."

---

1   French translation: "A lone person is always in bad company."

Hives wasn't budging. "Schoolwork comes first. It's my duty to make sure you complete this year without incident. That was the promise I made to your parents before they left for parts unknown. And I am nothing if not a man of my word."

Lala took a long, deep breath. "I have to use the restroom. *Now*," she snapped.

"What's she doing?" Boob asked in a hushed tone.

"Be quiet and watch a master at work," Rube replied.

Lala had all kinds of clever tricks up her sleeve. She grabbed her midsection and began convulsing. "Ugh!" she bellowed. "My bladder is filling up, and I don't know how much longer I can hold it. Better find a restroom fast or I might mess up these luxurious leather seats. You don't want *that* to happen, do you, Hives?" Lala was good at wiggling out of things. Her level of commitment to even the littlest of deceptions was both hypnotizing and enviable.

"Oh, for heaven's sake," Hives grumbled. *SCREEEECH!* He turned the car around in an instant and pulled into the Inside Scoop parking lot. "Pocketbook, please," Hives said, extending his palm. "A preventative measure to make sure you do not dillydally."

Lala smiled as she handed over her cash-filled clutch. "Thanks for always looking out for me, Hives." She swung the door open to find a horde of kids waiting in line for the hottest hot dogs and the iciest ice cream in town. "C'mon, boys." The trio exited the car, closed the door behind them, and made their way toward their destination. "Ha! As if taking my money away would stop me from getting what I want. Order as many hot dogs as you like, gentlemen. And tell them to put it on my account."

The Inside Scoop had been *the* hangout for Beechwood Middle School students ever since they'd gotten kicked out of their previous hangout, Mama Rigatoni's Pizza. After years of spitballs, soda spills, and stingy tipping, Mama Rigatoni had reached her limit. The Inside Scoop was better anyway. It was a small snack shack with outdoor seating as far as the eye could see. No one really cared that the food wasn't all that great. It was all about the vibe. Lines were always long, but they moved fast. On this particular day, the place was packed to the gills with soccer teams, band members, and youth groups. Even the Mathletes made an appearance. Everyone's eyes were fixed squarely on Rube.

"It's really crowded," he complained. "Maybe we should grab our food and go?"

Celebrity wasn't something Rube wanted. Sure, it made him feel good when people told him they liked his work, but ever since the Contraption Convention, some of his classmates looked at him differently. *In a bad way.* Memes of Rube and his machines floated around school. Some of them were actually hysterical. Others . . . not so much. Kids talked about him like he was a *thing* and not a real live person with feelings. He hated to admit it, but sometimes being the center of attention was cool. It made him feel important. But not always. *Too many eyes on me? No, thanks.* Being small-town famous was fine for the moment, but the only thing Rube truly cared about was building machines that solved problems in the most interesting ways possible.

"Hot dogs are made out of pig genitals, FYI," Boob whispered.

Lala cringed. "That's disgusting."

"It's true," replied Boob. "Meat companies take all their scraps, including pig genitals, and grind them into a thick pink paste. They squirt the goo into wiener casings, and then we eat 'em. In my case, a lot of 'em."

Rube, Lala, and Boob walked to the back of the long line, where they waited patiently to place their order. *Too many people staring at me. I feel like a sitting duck!* There were kids there who'd gotten sprayed at the garden unveiling. Now they were damp and giving Rube the stink eye. When one of them made eye contact, Rube nodded and flashed an apologetic grin. *I'm just as embarrassed as you are.*

There was a general lack of adult supervision at the Inside Scoop, which made some kids behave like animals. Mike and Ike were no exception. They crept up on either side of Boob, towering over him like twin refrigerators. Rube thought about stepping in and telling them to get lost, but the amused look on Boob's face told him his help wasn't needed.

"Well, well, well. Doctor Jockenstein's monsters have returned. The boys who share a brain!" Boob said. "Here for the buy-one-get-one-free special? Or are you hungry for another classic McNutt zinger? Grab a plate! 'Cuz I'm *always* serving."

The twins' mouths were covered in strawberry ice cream, like beasts that had freshly feasted on a rotting animal carcass. If rotting animal carcasses were made of ice cream. Their hands were sticky and their tongues electric green from munching on the gummy worms they always kept in their pockets. Having parents who ran a candy company meant Mike and Ike were always intoxicated by some kind of sweet substance. Mindless, unpredictable sugar monsters, forever searching for their next victim.

Mike grabbed Boob's arm forcibly. "You wanna go? Then let's go, McNutt. I'll fight you anytime, anyplace." Ike pulled his phone out of his pocket and started recording. *His signature move.* "This is gonna be good."

As the boys prepared to make their move, something miraculous happened. They stopped dead in their tracks, completely paralyzed with fear. A small honeybee had begun buzzing around

Ike's head, headed for his ice cream–soaked mouth.

"No!" Ike shouted, batting angrily at the air as the bee circled him. "NO! Stop that!"

"Get it away from me!" Mike screeched, flailing his arms in all directions.

The bee was undeterred. It wanted that sweet, creamy nectar that was slathered across the twins' faces. Boob stood perfectly still as Mike and Ike swatted at their tiny attacker, never once making contact. They did, however, slap themselves in the face more than a few times. All told, it was a chaotic and embarrassing sight. A small crowd gathered to observe the pandemonium, but one among them had seen enough. Reina Lopez calmly walked over, reached into the flailing pile of anarchy, and scooped the tiny bee into the palm of her hand, clutching it tightly so it wouldn't escape.

"For crying out loud, ya big babies!" she exclaimed. *"It's just a bee."*

"Get that thing away from me!" Mike screamed. "I'm serious. Get it away!"

Reina moved her clenched fist close to his face. "What's the matter? Afraid it might sting you? Maybe you should have *buzzed off* when you had the chance."

"Leave him alone," Ike warned. "You . . . you . . ."

"Jealous, big boy? You want some too?" Reina waved her fist

in Ike's face, relaxing her fingers just enough for the bee to poke out. *"To bee or not to bee, that is the question."*

"Don't!" Ike exclaimed. "I'll call my mom and she'll call her lawyer and they'll sue you!"

As the brouhaha grew increasingly chaotic, Lala slowly backed out of the scene to check her DMs. "I didn't come here for *this*," she said, positioning herself away from the conflict. But not *too* far away. She still wanted to see what happened next, albeit from a safe distance.

The twins were positively terrified. Rube and Boob were in awe; they couldn't take their eyes away. Neither of them knew Reina all that well since she was a new kid in school. *Kind of.* She'd grown up in Beechwood like everyone else, but a year ago she had gone by a different name and used different pronouns. That gender identity hadn't felt right to her. From what Rube heard, it felt pretty bad. *I can't even imagine.* Instead of living in fear and pain, Reina had decided to do something about it and, with the support of her family, embraced her truest self. The shy kid in the corner, too fearful to speak up, was gone. Now she was a glowing young lady, ready to tackle anything that came her way.

"This is not a good look for you, Ike," Reina observed. "I gotta be honest."

Reina's classmates were overwhelmingly accepting of her transition. Some had questions, mostly about her hair and style choices. Others were a little confused in general, but Reina didn't mind explaining her situation. A quick chat always seemed to do the trick. She was making new friends all over the place, though Mike and Ike, being disrespectful little ingrates, thought it was funny to call her by the wrong name, among other nasty things. Reina did her best to ignore them, but sometimes a little confrontation was just what the doctor ordered.

"D-d-d-do you want to fight or what?" Mike asked, his legs trembling ever so slightly.

Reina rolled her eyes. "I have a green belt in tae kwon do, fool. If I wanted to fight, you'd be down for the count already. What

I want to know is, who hurt you?" The twins squinted their eyes and furrowed their brows. They didn't understand the question, so Reina clarified her inquiry. "The two of you treat everyone like garbage. You *badger*. You *harass*. You *belittle*. You smell like sweaty cotton candy too, but that's beside the point. I just want to know what your problem is. So?"

The twins weren't sure how to respond. No one had ever confronted them like that before. They felt exposed and didn't like it. *At all.* Unable to think on their feet, neither of them had anything remotely resembling an answer. So they stayed awkwardly silent, scowling into the middle distance.

"Suit yourself. But if someone is hurting you, you should speak up. And if you're being jerks just to be jerks, that's really screwy. Either way, you know where to find me if you want to have some real talk." Reina strolled over to the grassy area nearby and opened her palm. Despite being free, the bee decided to explore her hand for a bit. "Take your time, li'l buddy. You're safe now."

Rube nudged Boob. "The twins are allergic to bees. File that information away in case we need it later," he muttered.

Ike overheard the comment and interjected, "We're *not* allergic."

"We just hate bees," Mike added with an embarrassed shrug.

"Wipe your mouths and stop harassing people, you slobs,"

Rube said, tossing a handful of napkins at the twins. Boob ran over to Reina to see if she was all right.

"That. Was. Amazing." His eyes widened when he noticed Reina's palm wasn't swollen or red. "It didn't sting you," he gasped. "Are you a bee whisperer?!"

"Nah. It knew I wasn't a threat, so it didn't feel the need to sting me. Bees are smart like that."

Boob was in awe. "The way you absolutely *dismantled* Mike and Ike was . . . *chef's kiss*! A flawless takedown. Ya know, those two morons have been hounding me for years. Took me a while to find the nerve to give it right back to them, but *you*? You floated in and owned them from the jump. What's your secret?"

"No secret. My uncle is a therapist, and he says people who've been hurt turn around and hurt other people. Maybe that's Mike and Ike? I don't know. I just want them to stop being so rude to everyone."

"Makes sense."

"Nice comedy act today, by the way. Some solid LOLs."

"You were at the garden thing? I didn't see you."

"Of course you didn't. I'm a shape-shifter." Reina watched wistfully as the bee zigzagged away into the sky. "And now my work here is done." She walked over to her bike and climbed on board. "Nice chatting, but I've got other things to do."

"Like what? Can I come? I'm into doing things. Or I can just watch. Whatever! You tell me." Reina put her helmet on and took off down the street. "Hey! Can we be friends?" Boob called out.

"Maybe!" Reina hollered back. "But don't make this weird!" She was already halfway down the block.

Boob's heart was full of admiration and curiosity. Sadly, the feeling wouldn't last. As he turned around and began walking back to Rube, he noticed a new player on the field: Zach Billingsley. "What's *he* doing here?" Boob grumbled to himself.

Lala reemerged now that the ruckus was over. "That Zach kid has bad vibes. Something I *really* do not want around me right now," she said to Boob. "I'm going to go see if we can cut the line. This place is getting to be a little *extra* for my liking."

Rube was pleased as punch to have run into Zach. "Hey! Look who I found!" he said, cheerily motioning for Boob to join them.

"Here we go." Boob put on a happy face and pretended everything was hunky-dory. "Hey, Zach. How's it going?"

Zach responded by punching Boob square in the chest in what he thought was a playful way but was actually super annoying. "Not bad, McNutt. Not bad at all."

A recent transfer student from parts unknown, Zach was a little dangerous and a little rude. He and Rube had bonded over their love of machine-making after a short stint in detention together.

Long story. Don't worry about it. They started hanging out every day, which caused Rube to push his other friends away. Pearl and Boob had felt slighted, and when the Contraption Convention rolled around, things had taken a weird turn. It seemed Zach had stolen Rube's designs and sabotaged the entire event just to make himself look good. *Then things took an even weirder turn.* Rube had ended up building a machine that uncovered the real culprit behind Con-Con's destruction. His science teacher, Mr. Blank, had been revealed as an international criminal mastermind named Professor Zeero. In the end, Zach was exonerated of any wrongdoing and Rube was hailed as a hero. Even though there were lingering questions about some of Zach's odd behavior, Rube wasn't interested in finding their answers. In his eyes, Zach deserved a second chance. Boob wanted to feel the same way, but he just couldn't bring himself to like the guy.

"Sorry I couldn't make it to that garden thing," Zach lamented.

Boob wasn't letting him off the hook. "But you're *here*, which is odd, since 'the garden thing' ended just a little while ago. The timing is kind of tight, don't you think? Seems like you could have made the effort. But I guess some things are more important than friends."

"I was actually waiting around for my mom to pick me up 'cuz it was supposed to be our first weekend together in six months. But she bailed. Like she always does," Zach explained. "So I came here instead, since I figured this was where everyone was going to be."

"Oh," Boob said, slightly embarrassed that he'd grilled Zach so hard. "Sorry to hear that. Hot dogs and ice cream should def fill that void."

The tension between Boob and Zach made Rube deeply uncomfortable. *Can't we all just get along?* But there wasn't much he could do about it. *Sometimes friends and other friends don't always hit it off.* Boob had been Rube's BFF for a million years, but Rube and Zach shared a unique bond, seeing as neither had a mother figure around, albeit for very different reasons. *Mine is dead. His is absent.* They understood each other in a way no one else did.

"Ugh! The manager said I have to wait in line like everyone else," Lala grumbled. "Now I really do have to use the bathroom."

"*Lala Palooza*," Zach said, leering. "You're so much prettier in person than in the pics people post online." *Whoa. Not cool.*

"Thanks. Shouldn't you be in a juvenile prison?" Lala shot back. "Or is your *runaway chic* look actually intentional?"

Zoinks! To avoid escalation, Boob brought the conversation back to its original subject. "Just use the bathroom here, Lala," he suggested. "It's what you told Hives you were doing anyway."

"You can't be serious. That thing smells like strawberry air freshener and poop. Sorry, I don't know what I was thinking coming to this zoo during *feeding time*. Enjoy the walk home, boys! The cardio will do ya some good." And with that, Lala departed, leaving Rube, Boob, and Zach to face one another in quiet discomfort.

"I don't trust that girl," Zach said. "With all her money, she can do anything she wants. She expects us to believe she wants to hang out with us regular people? Smells like a secret agenda to me. Bet she's up to no good."

"Lala is cool. I've known her a long time, actually, and she's not like that at all." *Change the subject, Goldberg. Unity, unity, unity.* "Hey, I was thinking maybe the three of us could get together and build a machine sometime? There are plenty of problems to solve. We could make lists, gather parts, corral a bunch of snacks. Make an event out of it."

"Great idea! Let's do it at your place, Zach," Boob suggested. "None of us have seen where you live, and it would be cool to finally meet your family. *If* they exist."

Boob, stop trying to start trouble. Rube knew his friends had reservations about Zach, but managing their expectations was too much work. *They'll just have to get over it. Zach is my buddy and everyone will eventually become friends. They have to! Right?* But some of the things Zach did and said drove Boob positively mental, and the only way he could address them was by being shady, which always destabilized Zach in some form or fashion.

"Oh, uh, my dad won't let me have people over," Zach said as a bead of sweat dripped down his forehead. "He's really strict about that kind of stuff. No friends, no visitors. We should do it at Rube's house, since his dad is away on a business trip." He raised his eyebrow mischievously. "Or we could just have a party instead..."

"No can do. My dad flies home *tonight*." After what seemed like an endless business trip, Rube's dad, Max, was finally on his way back to Beechwood. He'd been looking forward to his return for weeks. *I can't wait to see him! It's gonna be so awesome.* "So, yeah, sorry, but no parties."

"Oh. Well. That's a bummer. Hope he had fun in Arizona," Zach replied. "We'll just have to try again next time your pop leaves his party palace unattended. Hehehe."

Boob nudged Rube. Rube nudged Boob.

Zach was a strange and curious dude.

CHAPTER 3

"Honey, I'm home!" Rube shouted.

Why do people in old-timey sitcoms always announce them-selves like that? Who doesn't hear their front door opening and closing?! And don't they have security systems?!

With Max always away on business, Rube liked to entertain himself whenever he walked in the door. It made him feel less lonely, even though technically he wasn't alone.

Sniff, sniff. Boob's nose detected baked goods. Despite having already stuffed their faces full of hot dogs and ice cream earlier in the day, the boys couldn't help but hunger for more goodies. Boob pushed past Rube, ran down the hallway, and found a special guest dropping off a present in the kitchen. "Grandma Etta! My favorite gal in the world. Cooking up a storm, I see. And looking *sassy* as h-e-double hockey sticks. *Raowl!*"

Why does he flirt with my grandma when he knows it skeeves me out?

"Oh, Boob! Watch your language, you little *flatterer*," Etta said with a giggle. "Check out my new track suit, huh? It's velour. Very luxurious. Only twenty-five dollars from the Bargain Channel!"

A bubbly and vivacious personality, Grandma Etta had a style all her own. Her voluminous white hair was extra frizzy, turning her head into a giant puffball. Etta had a preference for gold jewelry, always wearing gilded necklaces, bracelets, and rings. Though her claim to fame was her long, brightly colored nails, which often had a unique style element. Seashells, Picasso, and the New York Mets were her favorite nail designs. "I like to be different!" she always said. Though she had a reputation for being a sweetheart, Grandma Etta was no pushover. Not by a long shot.

"As usual, you look like a million bucks, Grandma Etta. No. *Two million*," Boob replied. He was laying it on extra thick. "Red is, was, and will always be *your* color."

Etta showed off her spangly jeweled bracelet. "You like my summer diamonds?" she asked. "*Some* are diamonds, *some* aren't. Ha! Get it?"

Boob's face was aglow with admiration. "We stan a comedy queen."

Rube rolled his eyes. "Hand me a barf bag and *please* stop flirting with my grandma."

"*Never,*" Boob said. "You're lucky. My grandparents died before I was born. All I have are mean aunts with chopped-liver breath." He'd been eyeing a plate of freshly baked pecan cookies, waiting for the perfect time to strike. Now that Etta was nice and relaxed, Boob slyly inched his hand toward the fragrant dish as inconspicuously as possible.

"Don't even think about it, sweet-talker," Etta growled. She slapped his hand away and moved her darkly tinted glasses down to the tip of her nose so Boob could see the whites of her eyes. "If you lay one of your grubby little paws on these cookies, I'll slice it off, fry it, and feed it to you for breakfast tomorrow with a side of hash browns. *Capisce?*"

Boob nodded. "Yes, ma'am."

"Coming in here thinking you can butter me up and take whatever you want . . ." Etta said, shaking her head in disgust. "I was one of *seven kids.* I know *all* the dirty tricks. Thanks for the compliments, wise-ass, but keep your hands where I can see 'em."

Rube adored his grandma Etta's fierce sense of humor. *She doesn't put up with crap from anyone.* Her stellar cooking abilities were the envy of every old lady in the neighborhood. Rumor had it Etta's turkey chili recipe was so in demand, the other grandmas once tried to have her bumped off so they could steal it.

"Get over here, bubbala!" Etta exclaimed. She latched on to Rube, hugged him close, and kissed him on the forehead repeatedly. *"I can't get enough of my Rubey!"*

Years ago, after Rube's grandpa Papa Joe had passed away, Etta had been heartbroken. Living in an empty house full of memories in a faraway town wasn't easy, so she sold the place and moved to a tiny cottage in the corner of Rube's backyard. *Dad built it with his bare hands!* Now Etta was near the family while also having space to do as she pleased. At first it had been tough for her, feeling lonely without Papa Joe, but she soon realized he wouldn't have wanted her sitting around all day missing him. He'd want her to be active and happy. So Etta got her keister in gear and involved herself in all kinds of community affairs. When she wasn't walking around the partially abandoned mall, she was serving meals to the homeless, volunteering at the animal shelter, or spending time in nature. *Or napping. She loved a good afternoon nap.* Etta's second-favorite thing was playing mah-jongg with her Tuesday Ladies Club. Her first-favorite thing was leaving food in the fridge for Rube when Max was out of town. Most of the time, Etta and Rube were like ships passing in the night, but sometimes, when the timing was right, they collided in a brilliant burst of love and affection.

"I haven't seen you for days, Rubey. How's school? You doing your homework? Tell me everything!"

Why do adults always ask these questions?! Get some new material. Rube debated whether or not to tell her the truth. *School sucks. Just kidding. Kind of. Not really. Maybe? Okay, fine. School is . . . better than it has been?* After weeks of not studying, not doing homework, and being distracted with extracurricular machine-making, Rube's grades went south. *Fast.* However, in recent weeks, he'd begun to turn things around. A few B+ tests had put him on a new path. If he kept his head down and did the work, he'd be able to pull off a miracle and raise his average. Homework was still a soul-sucking chore and he couldn't concentrate to save his life, but there was hope on the horizon. *Sometimes that's enough to keep ya going.*

"School's fine," Rube said. "Can I have a cookie, please?"

"Anything for my little pumpkin boy," replied Etta. "I call him that because when he was a baby, he had the roundest little pumpkin tushie!"

Oh god. Make it stop.

Boob threw his hands in the air. "Hey! Excuse me?! HELLO?! How come he gets a cookie and *I* don't? *I'm* a little pumpkin boy too!"

Etta ignored Boob's outburst. She grabbed Rube's chin as he munched on his treat, pulling his face close to hers. "My sixth sense is pinging. There's something you're not telling me. Don't pee on my leg and tell me it's raining, Rueben." *What kind of old lady-language is that?!* "Is some jackass at school giving you a hard time? I swear, if it's those potato-shaped twins, I'm coming down there and kicking their butts tomorrow!"

"Here's the abridged version," Boob said, cozying up to Grandma Etta. "Rube made a machine for Pearl, but it backfired, and now everyone thinks he's a fraud. But you didn't hear that from me." He inched his fingers toward the plate of cookies like a fleshy spider about to attack.

C-CAW! C-CAW!

Without warning, Grandma Etta's pet parrot, Oberon, zoomed through the room, brushing past Boob and giving him the fright of his life. The feathered creature landed on Etta's shoulder, leaving a trail of tiny plumes scattered on the floor below.

"That thing almost gave me a heart attack!" Boob shouted.

Etta tilted her head against Oberon's wing, cuddling the bird lovingly. "What a good boy you are, Obie," she cooed. "You,

Boob, are a *bad boy* without any manners. What, were you raised by warthogs?! If you want something, *use the magic word*."

"Squawk! Boob is a bad boy!" Oberon cried. "Use the magic word! Squawk!"

"Can I have a cookie, *please*?" Boob asked sheepishly. Etta moved the plate in his direction. Boob gave it a once-over before selecting a small gooey treat and stuffing it in his mouth. "Mihshun agramplishhht," he chomped.

"*Good boy*," Etta said with a sweet smile. Suddenly there was a playful glint in her eye. "Just remembered a funny thing! Once when Rueben was a baby, he climbed up onto the counter when I was making lasagna and poured a whole jar of tomato sauce in his diaper. We called him Mr. Saucy Pants. HA!"

Etta had a knack for telling embarrassing stories at random times. Boob had heard most of them before, but this one had him shrieking in amusement. Rube wasn't laughing, though. He was barely paying attention. His unblinking eyes stared out the window.

"Hey. What's going on in that noggin of yours?" asked Etta. "I see the wheels turning. If something is eating at you, it needs to come out. Tell me all about this garden party hubbub."

I don't want to talk. The last thing Rube wanted to do was discuss failing in front of a big group of people and potentially dooming his friend's chances of winning her election. *I'm embarrassed.* And not just because his machine had gone haywire, but because Pearl might be mad at him. That stung more than anything else. *Grandma Etta doesn't understand.*

"I know what you're thinking," Etta said. She was laser-focused on Rube. "You don't want to talk. You're embarrassed. You think I don't understand . . ." *Is she psychic?!* "But listen, I've *seen* it all. I've *done* it all. I once talked a carjacker into surrendering! True story. Nothing fazes me! I've been on this mudball way too long to put up with bull honky. I'm so old, my underwear should be in the Smithsonian . . ."

Gross. Why is she telling me this?!

"I'm telling you this because I've failed too. We *all* have. It's part of life! But you can't let it get to you. Build another beautiful, ingenious gadget thingy and everyone will forget about the last one. People have very short memories. Sometimes that's a good thing. Sometimes not. Besides, who cares what people think? Screw 'em! Rueben, your brain is a gift from God. Don't ever forget that." She lovingly kissed Rube on the cheek. "I know it's hard to be a kid. I was one myself a million years ago. But you'll be peachy keen no matter what. *Promise.*"

"Thanks, Grandma Etta," Rube said. *That wasn't so bad, was it?*

Etta slid a piece of paper and some cash in Rube's direction. "My schedule has been cuckoo lately, so here's a list of groceries I need *you* to pick up this week. There's a vegan yogurt I've been dying to try. Get one for yourself and we can have a snack date!"

Mmmmmm, snacks. "Hey, Boob and I are gonna hang out. Wanna play board games and make prank phone calls with us?" Rube asked.

"Aw, honey bun, I wish I could, but I've got a gig. My dance team, the Movers and Shakers, are performing for those scamps down at the Veterans Hall." Noticing the time, she zipped up her purse and adjusted her outfit. "I gotta run! The other ladies'll rip me a new one if I'm late again. Listen up: There are pot roast sandwiches in the fridge, ready to go for dinner. Don't eat too many!"

"What time is Dad coming home?" Rube asked.

The question stopped Grandma Etta in her tracks, but Oberon spilled the beans before she had a chance to respond. "Squawk! Three more weeks! Squawk! Three more weeks!"

"Shush!" Etta snapped, tapping the bird's beak to quiet it. "Keep that yap shut or I'll stuff you in the oven. *Don't try me, bird.*"

"Oberon is wrong, though," Rube said. "The last time I talked to Dad, he said he'd be home tonight. He said *tonight.*"

"Sorry, bubba. Dad's plans changed." Delivering bad news to Rube was never easy for Grandma Etta. Whether it was revealing the hard truth behind the Easter Bunny or telling him brownies did not, in fact, grow on "brownie farms," it hurt her heart to see him crestfallen. "That wackadoodle job has him traveling all over the darn place. They yanked him down to Florida, then up to Maine. Now he's God knows where—"

"Phoenix," Rube said solemnly. "He's in Phoenix."

"That's right! Oof. He's been so many places lately, I can barely keep track."

Not Rube. He kept track of everything. He knew every city, state, airport, and hotel his father had been in for the past two months. He had confirmation numbers, flight numbers, and rental car locations. *Among other important information.* Rube made his dad text him every single bit of data. *Just in case.* When Rube had asked what time his dad was coming home, all he'd wanted was a simple confirmation. Instead, he'd been thrown for a loop.

Etta gave Rube a final kiss on the cheek and jogged to the front door. "All right, bubbala. I gotta go. Love you to the moon! Don't wait up!" And with that, the illustrious Grandma Etta departed, leaving the aroma of her sweet perfume (and pecan cookies) lingering in the air.

"Man, she really makes the world a better place, doesn't she?" Boob said. He put his hand on Rube's shoulder. "Look, you've waited this long, right? Three more weeks isn't *too* bad."

"Yeah." Rube's voice was soft and sad. *But I really miss my dad.* Then, like a message from beyond, he noticed a big brown box on the kitchen table, addressed to him. *What's this?* He tore the thing open and found an abundance of riches staring back at him. "OH. MY. GOD." The unexplainable sight took his breath away. After years of fruitless searching, the one item he dreamed of owning had magically arrived on his doorstep. *"Do you know what this is?!"*

Boob peeked into the box. "Looks like a torture device."

Rube gently removed the item and placed it on the table. "This is an antique electric toaster from the 1920s. Model number one-seventy-seven. Made by the Estate Stove Company in Hamilton, Ohio. In perfect condition. An absolute *beauty*. I've been looking for this exact model for years! Watch." He carefully opened each of the toaster's four doors and presented the shiny silver contraption in all its glory. "Look at this gorgeousness. With the doors open, it looks like a weird mechanical bird taking flight. *And* it makes four slices of toast! FOUR. SLICES. OF TOAST."

Boob had seen Rube excited before, but never like this. "Take it down a notch. You're making your regular toaster jealous," he whispered.

"*Boob,* you *don't* understand . . ."

"All I see is a kooky old toaster that looks like a baby Transformer."

"You're not appreciating the construction!" Rube reached into the box, searching its insides with his hand. "There's no note or anything." While inspecting the outside of the box, he noticed something uncannily coincidental. "No return address, but the postmark is from Phoenix."

"Awww. I guess your dad knew he wasn't coming home today, so he sent this li'l guy to say he's sorry. That's sweet." Boob peered inside the box. "There's nothing in here for *me*, right?"

Rube was of two minds about the gesture. *On one hand, it's*

awesome to finally have my hands on this delicious mechanical marvel. *On the other hand, I really just want my dad to come home. Does he think giving me presents makes everything okay?* It was a pretty great toaster, though. *I know that! Don't you think I know that?*

RUFF! RUFF! RUFF!

There she is. The lady of the house had finally made herself known. Bertha, the family dog, had been banished to the backyard earlier in the day after tearing up one of Grandma Etta's old wigs. To pass the time during her exile, she had chased squirrels and dug holes in the flower bed. Now she was licking the window, trying to get Rube's attention. *She's quirky like that.* "I see you, girl," he said. "Just give me a minute."

So, what do I do now? Do I tell Boob to hit the road so I can wander around the house sulking because my dad isn't coming home? Do I give my opulent pity toaster renewed purpose? It would be perfect for a Gutter-Cleaning Machine I've been thinking about lately. Or do I stop feeling sorry for myself and chill out in the backyard with my best friend and my dog? The answer was clear. "Grab those pot roast sammies, Boob. We're tossin' the ball with Bertha."

"Wunderbar," replied Boob. "That's German for *wonderful.*"

Rube opened the back door, and Bertha bounded onto his chest, leaving dirty paw prints all over his clothes. "*Easy,* girl," he said, placing one small sammie on the ground. "For you, my queen. Don't tell Grandma Etta I gave you this, okay?" Bertha gobbled up the delicious bite as the boys retired to the patio for some rest and relaxation. "This is the life," Rube said, taking a big ol' bite of pot roast. It had been a minute since he and Boob had chilled out together, shot the breeze, and caught up on all the latest Beechwood Middle School gossip. "What's the word, B? Talk to me."

"Health class is cringey." Boob shuddered. "I slept through most of the lessons, so I only got bits and pieces. Did you know girls have an aunt named Flo who visits them once a month and makes them feel *horrible*? We also learned not to touch people who don't want to be touched. It's called *consent*. Oh, and they passed out water balloons at the end. I took five."

"What kind of idiot touches people who don't want to be touched?"

"Exactly! Unrelated, did I tell you I came up with another new alternate curse word?"

"Stop. You're *killing me* with these—"

"How does this sound? *Cricketbutter.* As in, 'Aw, cricketbutter! I just stubbed my toe!' or 'That guy just got the cricketbutter kicked out of him.'"

"Cricketbutter is NOT happening. Neither is dungmug or noodlebrick."

"Give it time, my child," Boob said, rubbing his hands together devilishly. "Give it time."

"Should I get a new hairstyle?" Rube asked out of the blue.

"Sure. If you want. What kind would you get? Short, like a military commander, or long and luxurious like a barbarian warlord?"

Rube released a long, thoughtful sigh. "I don't know."

"Is this because of Davin?"

The question caught Rube off guard. "What?! No! Why would you say that?"

"He's *dreamy,* and I think he has a crush on Pearl. She's probably going to ask him to the Switcheroo Dance, and I figured you'd be jealous."

"Tuh. Buh. What . . . ?" Rube huffed and puffed but his mouth didn't form actual words. *Am I jealous?* Normally he'd try his best to say exactly what was on his mind. *I'm not jealous.* Boob was, after all, his best friend. *Maybe I'm jealous.* They told each other all kinds of things without fear of judgment. *Why would I be jealous?!* But this time, for some reason, he just couldn't express himself. *I think I might be jealous.*

"At least she's not asking Zach," Boob said.

"What's your problem with Zach?!" Rube shot back. "The kid needs friends. He's new in town, and the way he talks about his dad and how his mom is out of the picture makes me think he's having trouble at home. You don't have to be BFFs with him on account of me, but cut him some slack. He's making the effort."

"If you say so," Boob said smugly. "And for the record, *I'm* making the effort too."

The boys sat in silence for a few minutes, tossing the ball to each other as Bertha watched attentively. Whenever things got a little heated between them, a minute or two of silent cooldown brought them back to a mellow place. Rube used the silence to think about all the problems that needed solving in the backyard. New machines began swirling around in his head. *A tree-pruner for Dad, and maybe a mechanical clothesline for Grandma Etta? Something to think about . . .*

"I'm not going to the Switcheroo Dance," Rube declared.

"Me neither," replied Boob. "I'd rather drink a bowl of mucus."

"I'd rather sit in a closet for an hour with a big piece of dog doo."

"I'd rather wear a hat full of baby vomit."

"I'd rather get a tattoo of a butt on my face."

"I'd rather get a tattoo of a face on my butt."

"No one asked you, huh?" asked Rube.

"Nope," Boob said, shaking his head.

"Me neither. Would you go if Reina asked?"

Boob's eyebrow lifted. "*You* saw that thing with the bee. She's an instant legend! We played soccer together in elementary school but never really hung out before."

"Reina is a badass. No question."

"People better respect her pronouns! Or they'll have to deal with me."

Rube grabbed a pot roast sandwich, handed it to Boob, then stuffed another down his gullet. "Let the record show, you never answered my question."

"I wish I lived in another universe sometimes," Boob said. "A place where everyone can be themselves and not have to worry about anything."

Uh-oh. What's rattling around in that brain of yours now, Boob?

"There's a whole *multiverse* out there, you know. Anything is possible."

"Oh yeah! Like alternate realities and stuff. Worlds where history is different . . . like in *Spider-Man*! But that's a scientific theory. I just need *one* universe with you, me, Pearl, and a few other people."

"We'll call it the Rube-i-verse!"

"I think you mean the *Boob*-i-verse."

"That sounds like a website I'm not allowed to look at," Rube said, chuckling. "Did you know scientists at NASA think there was probably intelligent life in our galaxy before us, but they destroyed themselves with technology like eight billion years ago?"

"Hold up. How could they have technology if they were before us? That doesn't make any sense."

"*Yes, it does.* They developed technology but didn't know how to use it, so they accidentally blew everything up! Like when you punch someone, just kidding around, but because you don't know your own strength, you end up hurting them. With great power comes great responsibility, my friend. I heard that somewhere."

"How do you know all this science stuff?!"

"I read."

"Huh. I really gotta start doing more of that . . ."

RUFF! After several minutes of patiently waiting for them to throw the ball to her, Bertha reminded the boys of her presence. Rube tossed the ball into the corner of the yard, where it ended up behind a bush, away from Bertha's grasp. She took off to retrieve it.

"What should I do to make it up to Pearl since I messed up her event?" asked Rube.

"Build her a machine that apologizes?"

"*That's not how it works.* My machines aren't like *that.* They each have a real purpose that's born from a problem that needs solving," Rube explained.

"Fine, fine, fine," Boob groaned. "Build a machine that bakes her a cake!"

"Ugh. I ate *way* too many pot roast sammies. If I even *think* about cake, I'll hurl."

"Yeah. My mom is gonna be mad I spoiled my dinner."

Dinner. Holy crap! Holy crap, holy crap, holy crap!

"BOOB!" Rube screamed, checking his watch. "I'm supposed to be at Pearl's house for an early dinner in fifteen minutes!" He launched out of his seat and started pacing furiously across the backyard. "She asked me a week ago but I forgot. Then today she said, 'See you later,' and I figured it was just, like, how people say 'See you later' when you go your separate ways, but she actually meant 'I will see you later because you are coming to my house to have dinner with my family!'" A nervous sensation fizzed inside Rube's stomach. *More anxiety bubbles. Fabulous.*

"How did it get to be so late? I mean, we *did* hang out at the Inside Scoop for a long while *and* take our sweet time walking home. And we *really* shouldn't have stopped by the gas station and loaded up on additional snacks. Oh! That reminds me. I've been meaning to tell you, we should hunt for arrowheads someday. I heard there are a bunch down by the creek—"

"Boob! I'm covered in dirt and I stink like a dog! *What am I going to do?!*"

"Want me to get the hose? I can spray you down like they do animals at the zoo?"

"WAIT!" Rube shouted. "I've got just the machine." He bolted upstairs to his bedroom, where salvation awaited. All he had to do was find it, which was easier said than done. Rube's closet was a certifiable disaster, filled with smelly clothes, machine parts, and toys he hadn't played with since he was five years old. Whenever he had to clean his room, he just tossed stuff in there willy-nilly. *Who has time to actually clean?* Now it had become a mountain of miscellany waiting to drown him. He cracked the closet door with care and peeped inside. *There you are, my beautiful baby. But how am I going to get you out?* Rube had found what he was looking for, but removing it wasn't going to be easy. *Nothing to it but to do it!* He grabbed pieces of the apparatus, yanked them out, and shut the door quickly. *Easy peasy!* The De-Stink-A-Fier had been miraculously liberated without incident. It wasn't his most ingenious creation, but it got the job done.

Boob was aghast when he checked in on Rube. "What the—?!"

"*Stand back,*" Rube warned. He fired up the De-Stink-A-Fier, and was bombarded by a storm of spicy body sprays. "That should do it," he said, emerging from the fragrant cloud. Now, having been properly cleansed of stink, Rube threw a new shirt on and raced back downstairs. Boob followed close behind. "Lock the door when you leave, B. I'm out of here!" Rube rushed outside, hopped on his bike, and rode off. Boob went to the window and watched him speed away.

"Now *the work* begins."

Once Rube was out of sight, Boob moved to the kitchen table and inspected the antique toaster. "How about you and I have some alone time?" He pulled out a small envelope with the Li'l Sleuthy logo on it. Inside was a tiny baggie of powder, an itty-bitty brush, and a roll of tape. Bertha curiously panted at his feet. "Rube thinks this is from his dad. Maybe, maybe not. But *we know better*, don't we, girl?" Boob gently brushed a thin layer of powder on every inch of the toaster, revealing a handful of distinct fingerprints. He delicately laid pieces of tape over each one and lifted the prints with the utmost care, placing them on notecards.

"Just like Li'l Sleuthy always says, life is a mystery, and *I'm* going to solve it."

CHAPTER 4

Rube stood in front of Pearl's house, hunched over with his hands on his knees, panting like a dog. *I've never ridden that fast in my life.* It didn't help that his stomach was filled with hot dogs, ice cream, cookies, and pot roast sandwiches. *Please don't barf, please don't barf, please don't barf.*

His anxiety bubbles began gurgling some more. *Why am I so nervous? Wait. Is this a date?! It can't be a date. It's just a nice visit with Pearl and her family. Now get your butt up those steps and ring the doorbell.* Drenched in sweat and smelling like cheap body spray, he made his way toward the front door until, suddenly, he realized he'd made a gross oversight. *I forgot to bring a gift!* Pearl's family wasn't expecting one, but Rube's mom always used to tell him, "When someone invites you over to their home for a meal, it's nice to give them a kind gesture of appreciation." *Nothing in my pockets but lint. What do I do?!*

Looking around the yard for ideas, he noticed Pearl's mom's flower beds. *What if I just . . . ?* Rube reached down and yanked a handful of flowers from the soil. *Voila!* He brushed them off and cleaned them up a bit so as not to give away their origin. *She'll never know the difference.* Rube took a deep, cleansing breath and rang the bell. *DING-DONG.*

The front door opened, revealing Pearl's younger brother, Isaiah, sitting in his motorized wheelchair, glaring.

"You're *late*," Isaiah said. His nose scrunched tightly. "Why do you smell like cotton candy and fish?"

"It's my fancy body spray. This one is called *Seashore Surprise.*"

"Surprise!" Isaiah exclaimed. "It's disgusting."

Isaiah was the dry wit of the Williams family. His deadpan delivery cracked everyone up. Unless, of course, it was directed at *you.* Isaiah had muscular dystrophy, which meant his body had trouble making protein that builds muscles. It had become increasingly difficult for him to get around, so the family had gotten him a motorized wheelchair a handful of years back. Since then, Isaiah's Halloween costumes had been the envy of every kid in the neighborhood. He'd been a starship, a sea creature, and a DJ with turntables. What was he going to be this year? Rumor had it the Batmobile was at the top of his list.

Isaiah welcomed Rube inside and closed the door behind them. "How *nice*," he said, noticing the freshly picked flowers in Rube's hand. "I look forward to seeing my mom's face when you hand her that lovely bouquet."

"You think she'll like them?"

Isaiah grinned. "Just try not to stink up the place."

Relax. Make small talk. Be yourself, weirdo. "So . . . what's new, Isaiah?"

"Not your sense of fashion, that's for sure."

Dang. He got me there. "Give me a break. I was in a hurry."

"What have you done to my flowers?!" Pearl's Mom, Monica, knew her handiwork a mile away.

"Oh, these? They're . . ." Rube racked his brain, trying to come up with a workable excuse. "I forgot to bring a gift, so I improvised," he said, sheepishly handing her the bouquet. "Sorry."

"I suppose I *did* need to do some pruning . . ." Monica winced before giving Rube a hug and a quick peck on the cheek. "It's good to see you, Rube. We're happy you're here."

"See? You're happy I'm here," Rube boasted to Isaiah.

Marcus, Pearl's dad, greeted them in the foyer. "Lookin' good, Rube. And smelling . . . interesting. Hey, when's your dad getting home? He and I need to play a few more rounds of golf before it gets too cold outside."

"He's not coming home for another three weeks."

"Ah. Bummer. Must be hard having him away so much. Listen, you know if you need anything, we've got you covered, right? Our house is your house," Marcus said.

"Thanks, Mr. Williams," Rube said. "I appreciate that."

"Xavier!" Marcus shouted at the top of his lungs. "Come say hello to Rube!"

Xavier, Pearl's older brother, was in high school. *And totally acted like it.* A few years ago, he hadn't minded hanging out with his younger siblings and their friends. *Now it's like we're nothing but peasants to him.* All he cared about were sports, cars, and being by himself. "Hey," Xavier mumbled from the living room couch.

"Make yourself comfortable, Rube. Pearl will be down in a minute," said Monica. "Isaiah, Marcus, come help me in the kitchen."

Rube stood in the foyer, admiring the house's modern architecture. *This place is so much better than mine. I wish I could just live here instead.* Marcus was an architect, engineer, and artist who had designed the family home to accommodate Isaiah's needs. It had wide halls and doorways so his motorized wheelchair could navigate easily. There was even an elevator in the back so Isaiah could get to his bedroom. Every time Rube visited, he noticed a new and interesting design element. Of all the rooms, Marcus's home office was his favorite place. *That's where the good stuff is.* He wandered down the hallway to give it a look-see. *Mr. Williams won't mind.* In addition to family photos and architectural awards, Mr. Williams's office was where he kept his paintings. The walls always had something new on display. This time it was a mural brimming with sea life in bold, electric colors. Rube had never seen anything like it. *Wow. This thing is absolutely gorgeous.*

Pearl popped her head in, startling Rube. "There you are," she said, a book tucked under her arm. "I finally finished writing my speech for the student government forum. I hate having to pitch myself, but all the candidates have to do it."

"I'm sure it's great," Rube said. "Want to run it by me?"

"Maybe later." She sniffed the air. "What's that smell?"

"*Me.* You like?"

Pearl pursed her lips. "Did you take a bath in sugar, then rub tuna all over your body?"

"No. Ugh. It's a discount body spray my grandma got me. I was in a rush and didn't have time to take a shower before I came over."

Pearl chuckled. "I'm just giving you a hard time. It's not *that* bad, I guess . . ."

Rube pointed at the mural. "Your dad's art is so cool."

"Knock, knock. Dinner is almost ready," Marcus said,

noticing Rube admiring the underwater painting. "Biodiversity is pretty amazing, right? The oceans are teeming with so much *life*. After we got back from our last little snorkeling vacation, I was so inspired, I just *had* to capture the vibe."

"There are so many different types of animals and creatures."

"That's what makes life great," Marcus said, grinning. "Pearl, did you finish your reading?"

"Yep," Pearl said. She removed the book from under her arm and placed it on a shelf.

"Good. We'll discuss it after dinner."

"What class is that for?" Rube asked.

"No class. It's just a thing my parents and I do."

Rube inspected the book's spine. "*Claudette Colvin: Twice Toward Justice*. Huh. What's it about?"

"Claudette Colvin was a hero of the Civil Rights Movement. When she was fifteen, she refused to move to the back of a bus and give up her seat to a white person."

"I thought that was Rosa Parks."

"Same thing happened to Rosa, but it happened to Claudette first. A lot of people don't know that. That's why my parents and I do a little history lesson each week. My dad has been teaching me about Black art and literature too," Pearl explained. "Stuff they should teach us about in school but don't."

Wait just a second here. What exactly are they not teaching us in school?! I should probably read my history textbook a little more, huh?

"DINNER!!!" Xavier yelled.

Rube and Pearl gathered with the rest of the family in the dining room, where a feast of roasted chicken, green beans, potatoes, and cornbread had been laid out. Despite having already eaten multiple times in the past few hours, Rube's mouth watered at the scent. *I'm going to regret this later, but I can't help myself. It all looks so good.*

As everyone sat down and dug in, Rube felt at home. The Williamses were like his second family, and it had been a while since he had enjoyed a warm, home-cooked meal with someone other than Bertha. It got him thinking about his mom and how clumsy she had been around the kitchen. He snorted a little remembering the time she had dropped a pot full of hot tomato sauce on the floor. *Looked like a crime scene.*

"You okay?" Monica asked. "I season my green beans a little differently than you might be used to. If it's too much—"

"They're great," replied Rube. "It's just . . ." *Don't say it, Goldberg. Talking about your dead mom will bring the whole table down. Talk about something else! Ask them if they're watching that new show,* Chicken Challenge, *where people dress up in chicken costumes and compete in athletic challenges. It's the most popular show in the country!* "I was thinking about how bad my mom's cooking was, and it made me laugh." *Or not.*

"Oh goodness!" Monica exclaimed. She put her napkin to her mouth and tried not to chuckle. "Your mom was one of my best friends in the whole world, but she couldn't cook a meal to save her life. In college she almost burned down our dorm room making toast!"

"I remember that," replied Marcus. "Max always said she poured a mean bowl of cereal, though. That's why he married her, haha. We had some good times back in the day."

Rube noticed Isaiah eyeing him from the head of the table. *What's he up to? I better get ahead of whatever he's planning.* "How's school, Isaiah? What's your favorite subject this year?"

"*Drama*," he replied. "Which reminds me. What are your intentions with my sister?"

Xavier snickered, but Pearl wasn't in the mood for antics. "Cut it out," she snapped. "This is not a *scene* or a *show*. Stop being thirsty for attention. It's not funny."

"It's a *little* funny," replied Xavier.

A phone began vibrating loud enough for everyone to hear.

"*Marcus*," grumbled Monica. "*No devices at the table.* You know the rules. You *made* the rules. *And* we have a guest."

"Sorry," he replied, reaching into his pocket and turning off his phone. "Work stuff is never-ending. My firm wants to build more accessible homes in Beechwood, but some developer keeps buying up property out from under us. It's *really* frustrating. This town is rich in untapped minerals and gas, which I assume they're trying to find. We have laws about that kind of stuff, but the town council doesn't seem to care . . ."

Isaiah rolled his eyes. "Yes, Dad, please keep talking about work. We all love to hear about what the town council cares about," he groaned. "Tell us more stories about *gas*."

Monica ignored her son's attempt at humor and turned her attention to Rube. "Pearl told us the garden unveiling was a big success today."

She did?

"And I hear everyone loved your fancy watering thingamajig. Congrats! You're turning into quite the local celebrity. We'll probably be asking for your autograph soon."

Rube looked over at Pearl, who was conspicuously silent. *Did she not tell them?* Against his better judgment, he went along with the ruse. "Yep. Everything went off without a hitch. The whole crowd stayed very dry. Very, *very* dry. What can I say? I've got that magic touch, and Beechwood Middle School just can't get enough. Hehe." *Don't pour it on too thick, dork.*

"Rube's machine broke down and sprayed the entire crowd with water," Isaiah revealed. "Everybody is talking about it online. Mike and Ike Kowalski took a ton of pics *and* a video. Wanna see?"

Pearl calmly put down her fork and addressed the table. "Despite a *minor* mishap, Rube's machine is primed and ready to accomplish the task it was built for, and the garden is better off because of it. End of story. Now, would someone please pass me the green beans?"

Marcus smiled. "That's a future sixth-grade president right there."

"*Dad*," Pearl groaned. "Don't jinx my chances. *Please.* I have a million things to do before the election."

"Isn't that dance coming up?" asked Xavier. "The one where girls ask boys?"

Here we go again.

"The Switcheroo Dance is *the* event of the season," Isaiah said.

"That's right," Xavier said. "We used to go down to the thrift store and find the ugliest suits they had just to make our dates mad. Good times."

Monica looked directly at Pearl, then at Rube. "So, are *you two* going?"

"Mom."

"I didn't mean *together*. Unless you want to. Or not! You know what? Forget it. You middle schoolers are all too melodramatic for me. I'll be over here minding my own business."

The family continued to make small talk as they ate, chatting about the kinds of things families chatted about at the dinner table. But Isaiah couldn't stop eyeing Rube, and it made him feel increasingly uncomfortable.

"Everyone at the elementary school is talking about how good you are at building machines," Isaiah said, stuffing a green bean in his mouth. "But I'm just not seeing it."

Everyone at the elementary school is talking about me? That's haunting.

"Not to brag, but building machines is what I do. It's my thing," said Rube. "I see a problem that needs solving, and I try to solve it using stuff I've got lying around. That's just how my brain works. What else do you need to know?"

"So, if we needed our dishes washed, *and we definitely do*, you'd just whip up a dishwasher?" Isaiah asked. "Or does the thought of building a contraption on the spot make you *afraid?*"

Don't take the bait.

"*Afraid?* Psssh. I can build *anything, anywhere, anytime.* I'd build you a dishwasher right here, right now, but I don't have any parts." Rube shrugged.

"There are ten boxes of junk out in the garage," Xavier offered. "Just cleaned the place. Good stuff in there too. Hoses, sports gear, pipes, wheels, all kinds of usable parts. Bet you could make a dishwasher in twenty minutes tops."

"Well, you know . . ." Rube was beginning to waffle. "That's great that you have all that stuff, and I'm sure I could throw something together on the fly, but I don't have my notebook on me. It's got my designs in it. Sorry."

"And we already have a dishwasher," replied Monica. "I paid good money for it."

God bless you, Mrs. Williams, you lifesaver.

"That thing hasn't been working right for months," Marcus countered. "I've got a ton of drafting paper that's perfect for designing, and honestly, from one artist to another, I'd love to see how you create one of your masterpieces, Rube. What do you say? You up for the challenge?"

I've been backed into a corner by my own chutzpah. There was nowhere to go but down the rabbit hole. "Let's do it," Rube said, a frozen grin plastered across his face.

What have I done?!

"This is going to be *in-ter-es-ting*," Isaiah said, rubbing his hands together like an evil villain watching his archenemy get tortured. "Let the games begin."

Marcus grabbed his drafting paper, and Xavier brought the boxes of junk into the kitchen. Pearl played the role of construction manager while Monica and Isaiah watched from the dinner table as work began. A few months ago, Rube never would've imagined he'd be building a machine in front of human beings, let alone his friend's family. Constructing his machines was a private thing. *Other people just get in the way.* Trial and error were part of the routine, but Rube didn't want *anyone* to see him fail. *People don't understand the process. They think everything comes together through magic or something!* Since his success at Con-Con, however, Rube felt more compelled than ever to share his gift with others and show them how he did what he did. The pressure may have been high for him to make the next big thing, but as long as his nose was to the grindstone, he was a happy guy. The more comfortable he got, the more open he was to assistance. He even let Xavier and Isaiah lend a helping hand.

Marcus was fascinated as he watched Rube work. "We artists have a unique way of looking at things. We see the world differently. That's what gives our work its flair."

"I guess," Rube said. "Sometimes I think I invent stuff to keep myself from going nuts."

"Join the club," Marcus assured him.

As the clock ticked down, Rube put the finishing touches on his latest contraption and christened it the Dishwasher. "Nineteen minutes, twenty seconds. Not bad," he said, wiping the sweat from his brow. Pearl and Xavier cleared the dishes from the table and loaded them into the machine. Rube double-checked his water source. "Everything looks good. Let's start this puppy up!" Proud of his feat, Rube turned on the machine and watched it go to work.

Marcus beamed as the Dishwasher moved. He was fascinated by all of its inner workings. Isaiah sat, arms folded, amused by the scene. He'd gotten exactly the show he'd wanted. After the machine finished cleaning its final dish, the Williams family erupted into applause.

"A job well done," Marcus said. But Monica wasn't convinced.

"Congratulations, *absolutely;* you set out to accomplish your goal, and you made it happen. But tell me again why you went through all that hard work to do something we already have a machine for? Seems like your time and energy could be spent on

other things, but hey, what do I know?" Monica glanced at the clock, noticing the late hour. "Thank you for a wonderful evening, Rube. It's always good to see you. But I think it's best you get home before it gets too dark."

After saying their goodbyes to Rube, the Williams family went their separate ways so he and Pearl could have a little private time together on the porch.

"Fall is coming," Rube said, taking in the night sky. "Gettin' brisker."

Listen to yourself, Goldberg. You awkward goon.

"I hope that wasn't weird, talking about your mom," Pearl said. "My parents have been reminiscing *a lot* lately. It's what old people do, apparently."

"No, it's cool. I like hearing stories about my mom. Makes me miss her less." *That's not exactly true.* "It makes me miss her more, actually. *At first.* But *then* it makes me miss her less. I'm just glad your parents didn't tell stories about *us* when we were little."

"Oh, you mean like when they used to pile us all into the bathtub together?" Rube's face turned bright pink. "Remember that one time you peed? Hahaha."

She's laughing. She's in a good mood. Now's the perfect time to apologize for messing up the garden event. Get it over with. DO IT.

"I'm sorry for messing up the garden event," Rube said. "I don't know what else to say other than that I dropped the ball."

"I knew you hadn't finished building anything as soon as you put up that tent."

"You did?"

"Yeah. I didn't want it to be true, and I trusted you'd get it done in the end, but I'd already prepared myself for disappointment. I know you, Rube. This isn't my first rodeo." *Wow. Pearl just assumed I'd let her down. That hurts.* "Don't worry, though. I'm over it. Now I can go back to stressing about school, my upcoming chess championship, and the election."

"I've been meaning to make it to one of your chess matches."

But you haven't yet, so why are you bringing it up? "I can't believe your garden club really went with *Greenhouse Guild* as their name. I like *Plant Patrol* so much better!" *She doesn't care.* "Just think of the uniforms." *You're really going for it now, aren't you, big mouth?* "Your logo could be a tricked-out Venus fly trap with blood dripping from its fangs. And you could wear proton packs, like in *Ghostbusters*! But they'd be filled with fertilizer and—"

"Why are you so frustrating?!" Pearl blurted out. The annoyance she'd been suppressing all day had come back with a vengeance. "And seriously, why didn't you have your phone on you this morning?! I thought you were dead or something!"

Rube patted himself down. "I always leave it at home. Why didn't *you* lift up the tent to see if I was under it?!"

Pearl smacked herself in the forehead. "*You put a sign on it saying DO NOT TOUCH.* Also—why would I ever assume you'd be under there sleeping, on a pile of dirt?!"

She has a point.

"You've got a point," said Rube. "I wonder what Davin would have done?"

What does THAT mean?

Pearl nodded to herself. The cause of Rube's insecurities had become crystal clear. "Wait! Let me guess. You think I want to ask Davin to the Switcheroo Dance. Is that it? You know, just because he's *handsome* and *kind* and *sweet* and *smart* and *honest* and *self-aware* and . . . did I say *handsome*?"

"Yes."

"Good. Because he is. He's *all* of those things." Pearl furrowed her brow. "And now I forget the point I was trying to make, so all I'll say is this: A dance where girls are supposed to ask boys is stupid and outdated. Anyone should be allowed to ask anyone at any time. Making it all about gender is whack."

"Yep. *Totally agree.* A hundred percent. You couldn't pay me to go to that stupid thing," Rube said, nodding in agreement. *But I'd go if you asked me.*

"Get a room, you two!" Isaiah shouted from his second-floor bedroom window. "I can see Rube's clammy hands from here!"

Suddenly, a neighbor woman stomped into the Williamses' front yard and yelled up to Isaiah in frustration. "Excuse me, young man! It's after eight P.M., and you need to keep the volume down! This is not the time for yelling!" she screeched.

"But *you're* yelling," Isaiah said calmly. "A lot louder than *me*."

"Sorry, Mrs. Schlafly," Pearl said. Isaiah shut the window, but the woman wasn't finished.

"You people are so loud all the time! *Loud, loud, loud.* This is a nice quiet neighborhood and we like it that way. You need to abide by the rules or leave!"

Do something to make her go away. Now.

Rube turned away from the action and began barking like a dog. "Don't come any closer, lady!" he said, looking at the woman again. "I've got a German shepherd over here who hasn't eaten all day. One look at you, and I can't promise he won't want a bite. Hit the road. It's the only way to save yourself." Rube turned away again, barking even louder this time. The disgruntled woman, confused by his bizarre actions, stormed off without further incident. *That'll teach her to mind her own business.* As soon as she was gone, Pearl fell into a fit of laughter.

"Hahaha. You're out of your mind, Rube."

It feels good to make Pearl laugh. "What was that all about, anyway?" Rube asked.

"Oh, that's just our racist neighbor."

"You say that like it's okay . . ."

"It's very much *not* okay, but there isn't much we can do about her."

"If she's racist, why don't you call the police on her?"

Pearl's face went all scrunchy. "Are you being serious? Her husband's a cop. He knows what she says and does. Which is to always complain about *us*. She complained when my dad built a tree house, telling us we needed permits even though *my dad is an engineer*. He *knows* about permits. She complained when my mom hung Christmas lights outside. She yelled at Xavier for leaving his bike in *our yard*. She yelled at *me* for setting up a charity lemonade stand. And she never yells at anyone else on the block. *For anything*. The Griswolds had a three-day pool party over the summer with music blasting until three A.M. every night and people sleeping in their bushes. Mrs. Schlafly didn't say a word about it!"

"Wow. She sounds like a word-I'm-not-allowed-to-say. We need to *do* something. She can't get away with this."

"We've already tried everything. It's different when you're Black, Rube," Pearl said. "You've clearly never heard of 'the talk.'"

"You mean the birds and the bees? *Everyone* has heard of that . . ."

"No, I mean the talk parents give their kids about being careful, always keeping your hands where people can see them, never making sudden moves, being extra polite when you speak to an authority figure even if you didn't do anything wrong . . ."

"My dad hasn't given me that talk yet."

"Because you're not Black." Pearl stared at the empty spot in her mom's garden where Rube had uprooted his bouquet. "You really came over here and ripped up my mom's favorite flowers? All that brain power, and that's what you came up with?"

"I didn't know what else to do!" Rube pleaded. "They'll grow back in no time. And hey, at least she's got a great daughter who's a Gardenatrix Supreme."

"Changing the subject . . ." Pearl said, her eyes lighting up with excitement, "I chose red, blue, and yellow for my campaign colors. Kind of a Wonder Woman vibe instead of the regular red, white, and blue. Just had a bunch of buttons printed up too. You want one?"

"Sure, but let's be real—this whole class president thing feels like nerd stuff."

"Ha! Yes, please, boy who makes machines out of trash. Tell me more about *nerd stuff.*"

"You know what I mean. Student council is about planning dances and decorating the gym for pep rallies. It's honorary. The school isn't giving *real power* to a bunch of preteens."

"Well, how about this? I'm going to change that. I'm going to make everything we do *count*. If we could start a STEM program, do you know how amazing that would be? Even a new paint job would go a long way. Little changes can make a big difference. Our school needs to be better. *You* need to be better too. Got a machine that can solve world hunger? Gonna build a contraption that fights climate change? I didn't think so." Pearl fished around in her pocket, found what she was looking for, and pinned it on Rube's shirt. "Have some flair. Show your support."

"An official PEARL HAS A PLAN button!" Rube said. "I feel honored."

"I'm not trying to get cocky or anything, but with no one running against me, the path to victory is all but assured."

Uh-oh. She doesn't know about Emilia. This is not good. Do I tell her? I can't. But what if she finds out I knew? Then she'll be mad. But maybe not. Okay, I'm going to pretend I don't know. It's better this way. I think. Ugh, what am I supposed to do?!

"Why did you lie to me earlier today?" Rube asked point-blank.

Where did that thought come from?!

"What are you talking about?"

"At the garden event. You looked at your watch and pretended like you were running late. But *that* watch is broken. Last year you told me you only wear it because you like the way it looks. So . . . ?"

Pearl eyes were cast downward. "I didn't feel like sticking around, that's all."

Rube nodded. "All righty then." *Ask her if it had something to do with Emilia. Wait! Don't do that. You might not like the answer. Best to get the heck out of here and drop it.* "Thanks for dinner and everything. See you at school tomorrow." *Good call. Leave now. Hop on your bike, go home, and obsess about all of this until you fall asleep.* Rube waved at Pearl as he rode away. *Sigh. Why can't growing up be easy?*

"How you are doing?" Marcus asked, joining Pearl on the porch. "Isaiah said Mrs. Schlafly was being a pain again."

"I'm fine," she replied softly.

"Sometimes this town reminds me there's so much work still to be done. Fear and racism wrapped in anger and topped off with jerk sauce. Not the tasty kind either. But we keep going, don't we?" He put his arm around Pearl. "Rube is a good egg. I'm glad you two are friends. But that boy *stinks.*"

They both laughed.

CHAPTER 5

"Ugh, I hate this!"

For some kids, gym class was the ultimate treat. They got to frolic and play sports instead of reading books and learning about important things. For Rube and Boob, it was a source of discomfort. A soul-sucking engine of anguish. *And that's on a good day.* It wasn't that they disliked physical activity, they just didn't want to experience it with their cockiest classmates. *We all know the type.* Take, for instance, Kevin Gallagher. He fancied himself the King of Athletics. The guy played football, baseball, basketball—all the basics. Was he good at any of those things? That was debatable. But it didn't stop him from critiquing everyone else's performance. In Rube's case, the critiques began before the game had even started.

"Hot tip, Goldberg. It helps if you actually *dodge* the *ball*. Haha!" Kevin cackled. In an instant, he'd rounded the corner and moved on to his next victim.

I wish I could throw a million dodgeballs right at Kevin's dumb face.

Being forced to spend time with kids you didn't particularly care for was just part of school. Getting hit with rubber balls of varying sizes was not.

"It's only forty-five minutes," Rube said softly to himself. "We'll be out of here before you know it."

The locker room was a miserable place. It was a dark, damp dungeon that reeked of prepubescent body odor. No one liked the place, but where else was everyone supposed to change? Each student was given a set of gym clothes to be worn during class. Then, after class, they deposited them in a bin to be washed. *Allegedly.*

"Not a fan of the tank-top-and-shorts look," Boob said. He inspected the labels inside each piece of clothing. There was a date written in black ink on all of them. "These are from 1995?! No wonder they're so cruddy."

Rube always felt exposed in the locker room, both literally and figuratively. It was an unavoidable consequence of puberty. But it wasn't all bad. At least he and Boob had each other.

Zach tossed his backpack onto the bench next to Rube. "Did you do the science homework last night?"

Uh-oh. Forgot about that. "Nah. I'll do it in between classes," Rube replied.

"Don't sweat it. You can copy mine." Zach put his arm around Rube in a warm and genuine way. "I've got you covered, buddy."

"Copying isn't really my style," Rube said. Though homework was a laborious chore, it was the doing that helped him learn.

"Are you worried you'll get caught?" asked Zach. "It's not like Mr. Blank is watching you like a hawk anymore. Oh wait. Sorry. I mean *Professor Zeero.*"

Ah, yes. The teacher who had been revealed to be a criminal and then taken away to who-knows-where. A totally normal thing that happens in small-town America.

"What do you think happened to that guy?" asked Boob.

"He's probably at a supermax prison upstate," Davin chimed in from the corner. "Or living on a faraway island in secret. Guys like that pay people off to get out of trouble."

"When I was locked up in juvie, this one boy was released early because his dad was some big-shot businessman downtown. Happens all the time," Zach concurred.

Locked up in juvenile hall!?! Zach is dropping bombs today.

"What were you in for, Zach?" asked Boob. "Disorderly conduct? Shoplifting?"

"Can't talk about it. My dad is a big-shot businessman downtown," Zach replied with a sprightly snicker.

Is he joking? He has to be joking. Right?

"What do you think *really* happened to Zeero?" asked Davin. "Be serious."

Zach kept his head down. "Honestly? Who cares?" he said, stuffing his school clothes into his locker. "I'm sure he's probably forcing someone to do his dirty work just like he did when he was a teacher."

"*Harsh,*" Davin replied. "I think you're just bothered 'cuz he was fixing to fail you."

"Might have *something* to do with it." Zach smirked, eyeing Rube with suspicion. "You never told us about that dude Professor

Butts. Didn't you say he was Professor Zeero's archenemy? Feels like you might be hiding something, Goldberg."

Rube gulped. He didn't expect to be put on the spot like that. *Why is Zach bringing this up now? Is he accusing me of a cover-up?* Having an older inventor pal named Professor Butts was fairly strange, and Rube knew it. The Professor just wanted to be left alone; he had revealed that even the slightest tidbit of information might blow up his spot. *Gotta play this one real smooth.* "Never hide Butts! That's my motto."

Everyone laughed, except Zach. His eyes were fixed directly on Rube. *He's not letting this one go, is he?*

"The Professor is an old friend of my dad." *Nice cover. Keep it going.* "*Was* an old friend of my dad. He's dead now. Butts, that is. Struck by lightning. Then hit in the head with a tree branch. He might've lived if that boulder hadn't rolled in out of nowhere . . ." *Now you've gone too far. Reel it in, Goldberg.*

"*Huh*," Zach replied. "And *how* did your dad know him?"

Stop with these questions already, dude. "School. They both went to school. Together. Not at the same time, because the Professor was older. It's actually not worth getting into. I'll tell you another time." Zach nodded. He seemed somewhat satisfied with Rube's perplexing answers. *But it's hard to tell with those stringy bangs covering his face.*

As more boys filed into the locker room, Boob became decidedly more nervous. He could hear Mike and Ike just around the corner, gossiping about something sinister. Though the twins had stayed relatively quiet since Reina had embarrassed them in front of everyone, Boob never knew when they might strike again. They were always plotting a new nefarious attack, and Boob was exhausted by the prospect of having to defend himself once again. All he wanted was to be left alone in peace. Now, in his most vulnerable state, he didn't have the energy to handle any of their bull. "Ugh, my stomach is doing cartwheels," Boob said. "Now that I think about it, it's better if I sit this one out."

Rube leaned over, talking low in Boob's ear. "Is this a Mike and Ike thing? If those two try to start anything, you know I've got your back."

"It's not that . . ." Boob trailed off, wondering if his ruse was even worth it.

"Don't stress, B. I already took care of it," Zach said. His tone was oddly confident. "You're good to go. *Trust me.*"

"Took care of what?" asked Boob.

PFFFFFFT! A relentless fart sounded from the other side of the locker room. *BRAMMMPPP!* Then another. *FFFFFSSSSST!* And another. Boob and Rube peeked around the corner to see what was going on. What they witnessed was both their best dream and their worst nightmare. Mike and Ike were keeled over, clutching their midsections. Something was happening inside them. *And it was not good.*

"I knew we shouldn't have eaten baked beans for a snack in between classes," Mike whined. "Why can't we stop eating baked beans?!"

Snackin' beans?! That's next-level gross!

Ike was paralyzed. "I think I had an accident." His eyes widened in embarrassment.

The locker room erupted in laughter that continued for a solid minute. *At least.* All Mike and Ike could do was clutch their

stomachs and be humiliated. Unable to help themselves, the twins stayed silent and waited for the feeling to pass.

Coach Brown heard the commotion from his office and stomped into the locker room to investigate. "My god! What is that stench?! Did someone squeeze a hippo to death?!" Noticing Mike and Ike in dire straits, Coach Brown made a command decision. "Both of you to the nurse's office. *Pronto*. And if anything happens to those gym clothes, you're paying for the dry-cleaning. Everyone else—let's go!"

In an instant, Boob's pretend stomachache went away like magic. "A bully-free gym class? I have been *reborn*!"

"Glad to hear it. Everything happens for a reason." Zach's sly smirk told a story.

Did he . . . have something . . . to do with this?

The boys slowly filed into the gym, making small talk as they went.

"What's everyone doing for the Switcheroo Dance?" asked Davin. "I mean besides dancing their asses off."

That stupid dance. Rube didn't want to talk about it. *Since I'm not even going*. But if he *did* go, he wondered if the occasion might call for a flashy machine or two. *You know, something lively and entertaining*. He envisioned a wonderland of fascinating contraptions for students to take photos with and operate. *Like a petting zoo! But for machines.* Rube was so distracted by his burst of creativity that he completely missed Coach Brown tossing a dodgeball in his direction. It hit him right in the stomach.

"Welcome to BROWNTOWN, Goldberg!" screeched Coach Brown. It was his famous catchphrase, which had new humorous meaning in light of recent events.

This is going to be the longest forty-five minutes of my life.

During other gym classes, Rube and Boob usually walked right up to their opponents and said, "Hit me!" so they could sit on the sidelines together and gossip. But today, feeling free and clear, they raised their game. Despite many tiring rounds of dodgeball, Rube survived by the skin of his teeth. *The trick is to stand behind the biggest kid so they get hit and you don't.* And Boob, in a shocking development, ended up having the time of his life. He and Zach teamed up on several occasions, bopping enemies when they least expected. Rube was happy to see his best friend and his new friend bonding. *Finally.* It felt like the beginning of something special. Later, at lunch, the three of them sat together, joking and laughing their way through every bite. *I like this. This is nice.*

"Anyone save me a seat?" Pearl asked.

Zach scooted over to make room. "Whatever you need is yours, future sixth-grade class president," he replied. Pearl blushed at the compliment. "How's the campaign going?"

"Good, good. Getting the word out. Hearing what students are interested in. But running for student government isn't just about what we *want*, it's about what we *need*. And we need transparency. We need to hold the people who run our school district accountable," Pearl explained. "But enough about *that*. I'm thinking about making temporary tattoos with my campaign logo to give out to people as a promotional item. Thoughts?"

"What about *real* tattoos?" Boob suggested. "*Of monsters.* I'll get a Cthulhu on my back. Or a Mongolian Death Worm! Whatever works best."

"Go big or go home. I like it," said Zach. "I'm gonna go grab another pudding cup. Those things are fire." As soon as Zach was out of earshot, a burst of gossip spilled forth.

"Zach, Boob, and Rube: the three musketeers," Pearl declared. "Did you guys sign a peace accord or something? I could hear the three of you guffawing from across the cafeteria."

"I was wrong about Zach," said Boob. *Whoa. What?!* "Being the new kid is tough. It's hard coming to a new school and making new friends. Heck, it's hard being at an *old* school and making new friends! Maybe he's not perfect, but he's cool in my book."

"Makes sense to me," Pearl said.

"Plus, with Zach not getting along with his dad, he needs people he can trust and confide in. Has the guy been flaky? Yes.

Rude? Definitely. But he did me a surprise favor today, one that I'm not asking too many questions about, and for that I'm forever indebted. I should at least give the guy a chance."

Pearl hadn't thought about Zach all that much. She had been suspicious when he and Rube had first started hanging out, but that was mostly because Rube had become obsessed with the Contraption Convention, leaving Boob the odd man out. But that wasn't Zach's fault. Boob's unexpected endorsement had Pearl seeing Zach through a different prism. If her friends were cool bringing him into their circle, she would be too.

Zach returned with an extra pudding cup and sat it in front of Pearl.

"Thanks," Pearl said. "That's sweet."

Hmmmm. "Sweet," eh? What exactly is happening here?

The look in Pearl's eyes told Rube she was about to do something unexpected. *Her rascally streak looks like it's about to rear its ugly head.* Like the time she had pushed Rube into the lake at day camp. Or the time she'd told the server at Mister McChucky's that it was Rube's birthday even though it wasn't and the waitstaff did their creepy birthday dance while singing to him. *She's going to try something on me, isn't she? Well, this time I'm ready.* Whatever was about to happen made Rube's heart flutter with inquisitiveness. He calmly sipped his water and stayed ready for anything.

"Zach, do you want to go to the Switcheroo Dance with me?" asked Pearl.

PFFFFFFFTTTTTT! Rube spat water across the side of Boob's face. *She did not just do what I think she just did.* Rube clumsily wiped Boob's cheek as they awaited Zach's response.

"Uh, yeah, that would be cool," Zach said, glowing. "I'd like that."

Pearl was ecstatic. "Awesome. Go big or go home, right?"

Just as Zach was about to dig into his new pudding cup, he realized he'd gotten the wrong flavor. "Butterscotch. Blech. What was I thinking? BRB."

As soon as he left, chaos broke loose.

"Traitor!" Rube exclaimed. "How could you do this to me?!"

Oops. Didn't mean to say it like that.

Pearl was taken aback. "Do this to *you*?!" She had no idea what Rube was talking about. "I asked Zach to the dance because he's part of our group now. Isn't that what you wanted?"

What I wanted was for you to be nice to him, not ask him to the most important social event of the semester! Not that I even care about that stupid dance, 'cuz I don't!

"Rube, you said—" Boob started to point out.

"Don't *you* start either. I know what I said!" snapped Rube. "So, what, are you and Zach best buddies now too?" He adopted a mocking voice to drive his point home. "*Oh, Zach, thanks so much for putting fart juice in Mike and Ike's water bottles! Now I can get hit in the face with dodgeballs in peace!*"

Pearl cringed. "I have no idea what you're talking about, but for someone who *literally* told us to give that kid a chance, your saltiness is not appreciated."

"I said *give him a chance*. I didn't say *ask him to the dance*," said Rube.

"Why are you getting so bent out of shape? You don't even want to go to the Switcheroo Dance," Pearl pressed. *You couldn't pay me to go to that stupid thing.* I heard you say those words. Don't play like you didn't."

"Well, *you* said a dance where girls ask boys is stupid and out-dated."

"It is! But I never said I didn't want to go," Pearl said, folding her arms.

Rube nodded. "So *that's* how it is?"

"That's how it *is*," replied Pearl.

"Fine. Do what you want. Have fun! Sorry I won't be there to see it." Rube put his arm around Boob. "*We're* having an anime marathon that night. At my house. With popcorn and two-liter bottles of every soda you can imagine. Right, B?"

"I didn't agree to that," Boob said. "But I do enjoy anime. And what popcorn flavors are we talking about? If cheese is on the menu, I'll need to bring my cheesy popcorn smock. Don't want to get orange fingerprints all over the furniture."

"Hrmph," Rube said, returning to his lunch a little miffed.

When Rube was distracted by his food, Boob whispered in Pearl's ear, "Keep your friends close and your enemies closer. I see what you're doing, and I applaud your efforts. We're in this together."

Pearl was perplexed by his disclosure and unsure how to respond. Thankfully, she didn't have to. Principal Kim walked through the cafeteria with a stranger, catching everyone's attention. Their pace was brisk and, from the outside, it looked as if Principal Kim was in trouble of some kind. His companion was an older, slick-looking business type. Tan with bushy eyebrows and a facelift gone wrong. His skin was crinkly like a snake's skin found in the woods after they shed it. The brown spray he had used to color his hair had mixed with his sweat, which dripped down his cheek in a strange formation. And he was headed in Rube's direction.

"Rube Goldberg." The man's voice was low and scratchy. Like he'd swallowed a chimney, then eaten a bunch of pebbles.

"That's my name," Rube said. "Don't wear it out."

Principal Kim's eyes widened. "This is *Superintendent Atwater*, Rube. *A very important person* who happens to be visiting us for a little while. He heard all about your triumph at the Contraption Convention and wanted to meet you. Isn't that cool?"

Rube didn't know how to respond. "Sure?" He shrugged.

"It's an honor to meet you," Atwater said, stone-faced. He'd joined the school district over the summer, but none of the students knew much about him, other than the fact that he drove a bright yellow sports car with a spoiler on the back and a vanity license plate that said IMAWNNR. *So gross.* Atwater was visiting Beechwood Middle School in an observational capacity. For how long was anybody's guess. Due to space issues, he was forced to share Principal Kim's office. Neither one of them seemed to like that very much.

"And this is Pearl Williams, one of my outstanding student assistants," said Principal Kim. "She recently oversaw our garden's makeover, in addition to being the school's resident chess champion *and* an exceptional Mathlete. Pearl is also running for sixth-grade class president. She does it all!"

"How nice," Atwater groaned.

Despite Atwater's rude reception, Pearl nodded kindly. Something told her not to let the moment pass. "Superintendent Atwater, I'd like to speak to you about the large monetary donation that Lala Palooza gave to Beechwood Middle School recently. As you know, sudden budget cuts scrapped our plans for needed renovations as well as a STEM program, which, to be honest, I was very interested in being a part of. Now that we *have* funding, can you confirm that these things will be handled in the coming months?"

Atwater looked at Pearl dismissively. "Smile more, little miss. You're young and have your whole future ahead of you. Adult business is none of *your* business," he said in a condescending tone. "The money is under my control. That's all you need to know. Best of luck with your little election."

Atwater was about to walk away, but that didn't stop Pearl from reminding him she was a force to be reckoned with.

"You'll be hearing from me again soon," she said, smiling from ear to ear. "Have a good day! And thanks for stopping by."

Atwater seemed beyond irritated as he strode off. Before Principal Kim chased after him, he silently mouthed an encouraging message directly at Pearl: "Keep up the good fight."

Those five simple words energized her like nothing else. Pearl knew she was on the right path and this was just the beginning. But another conflict loomed on the horizon. Emilia Harris was headed toward their table. Emilia had been branded a mean girl back in elementary school, which meant she and Pearl weren't exactly friends. They weren't exactly enemies either. But that was about to change. Kind of.

"Here," Emilia said. She carefully lifted an antique wooden box out of her canvas bag and handed it to Rube. "This is for you." He could barely believe his eyes.

"This is a nineteenth-century Jacot music box from Switzerland!" he gasped. "Rosewood . . . a floral design . . . in incredible condition . . . If it still has its original parts, I'm going to freak out . . ." Rube lifted the lid to find a disappointing surprise. Emilia had gutted the music box and replaced its precious insides with a crudely designed machine of her own creation. *Why would you defile such beauty?* Sadly, despite Emilia's obvious effort, the machine didn't work.

"Ugh!" Emilia sobbed. "It was supposed to do this whole thing where it whizzes and twirls and then a sign pops up that says . . ." She trailed off for a second. "Oh, never mind. I'm so stupid . . ."

"No, you're not," Rube assured her. "*Tell me.* What did the sign say?" Pearl and Boob were on the edge of their seats, crunching on banana chips as they watched the soap opera unfold.

"It was supposed to ask you to the Switcheroo Dance."

Oh. Oh my. Did NOT see that comin'.

"Sometimes things don't go the way you plan 'em." Rube shrugged. "Happens to the best of us." *Ouch, Goldberg. Insensitive much?*

"I really wanted to impress you since you're, like, this amazing machine guru, but I feel so stupid now."

A girl who just gave you a gift is crying in front of you. Do the thing you know will make her feel better. But what if I . . . ? STOP WASTING EVERYONE'S TIME AND DO IT.

"*Yes*," he said. "I'll go with you to the Switcheroo Dance."

Emilia's eyes lit up like a Christmas tree. "OMG. Really?!"

"Yep." *What did I just do?*

"Things are getting downright messy," said Boob. "And I am *here for it.*"

CHAPTER 6

Returning home after his strange day at school, Rube plopped himself on the couch and lay there, staring at the ceiling, while Bertha licked his face. It was just him, a fidgety pup, and an onslaught of thoughts. *They're icing me out. My friends teamed up to use my words against me in a vengeful way. After everything I did for them! After years of love and harmony! This is how it ends. So sad. I expected more. But alas, life goes on. At least Emilia cares. She seems . . . nice. Okay, you know what? These are actually screwy thoughts, and I don't like them. GO AWAY, SCREWY THOUGHTS. GET OUT OF MY HEAD AND NEVER COME BACK. Sigh. What should I have for a snack? Can humans eat dog treats? They look like sausage, so I'm thinking yes. NO, DO NOT EVEN TRY IT. BAD THOUGHTS, BEGONE! I need to get out of this house.*

"Yeah, this isn't gonna work for me, Bertha."

Rube sprang from the couch, grabbed Grandma Etta's grocery list, and made a command decision. *To the supermarket!* He

hopped on his bike and took off like a bolt of lightning, Bertha galloping beside him. *Leash laws? What leash laws?* Taking the scenic route was much more picturesque than riding down the main road, especially with the fall colors creeping in. Rube raced down the forest path, where leaves were beginning to scatter across the trails. He thought about the Lair and how he and his friends talked about going there far more than they actually did. It wasn't that they didn't want to. *That place is the best. The perfect clubhouse!* But time wasn't always on their side. The busier the school year got, the less time they had for adventure and exploration.

Coming out the other end of the woods and into the town center, Rube noticed something unusual. Many of the small shops and businesses had closed. *Places I've been going since I was a little kid.* Only cold, empty storefronts remained. No FOR SALE signs, no COMING SOON placards. Just hollow, vacant buildings. *Well, that's sad.*

Rube was shocked to find the building that once housed the largest collection of activewear in the tristate area had been torn down completely. *They got rid of the yoga pants store!* The now-empty lot was fenced off with a sign that said: KEEP OUT! PROPERTY OF THE NULL CORPORATION. *I hope they're turning it into a roller-skating rink. Or one of those bowling alleys that glows!*

Despite the somber sight of so many deserted buildings, Rube's fantasy engine couldn't help but think about the future. *I should open up an old-timey emporium. Or a museum of invention! I'll give demonstrations of my machines, and the gift shop will have keychains with my face on them. No, Bertha's face! And I'll do local commercials where I say, "Come on down!" and they'll give me the key to the city. How much does it cost to run a business? Oh well. I'll find out.*

BARK! BARK! BARK!

Despite all the town's changes, one of Rube's favorite places was still standing, and Bertha wanted to visit. The Treasury was an antique store Rube and his mom used to frequent back in the day. She had loved picking up trinkets and treasures for her collection of knickknacks, while Rube had loved playing with the old jukeboxes and vintage electronica.

"All right, girl," Rube said, leaning his bike against a tree. "We'll pop in and say hello real quick." Opening the door, he was greeted with one of his favorite scents. *The musty smell of history.* It was stale and dusty. *In the best way possible.* Rube loved antiques because they were filled with secret history and had lived countless lives.

"Well, look who it is!" exclaimed Herb Rosen. He quickly stopped what he was doing and summoned his wife from the back of the store. "Elanor! Come! We have a guest!"

The Rosens had opened the Treasury on a whim. Over the years, they'd acquired quite a collection of artifacts and relics. Many were family heirlooms; most were items they'd fallen in love with during their travels. Each piece had special meaning and a story to go with it. There were wedding gifts, awards, birthday presents, and remembrances.

When the Rosens had retired, they'd wondered what adventures might come next. Seeing as they'd been around the world and experienced the planet's many wonders, there wasn't much left for them to do, and life had quickly become boring. Herb and Elanor needed something to keep them active and engaged. Realizing their treasure trove of goodies was meant to be shared with the world and not cooped up in a drafty attic, they bought the old Helden Candy Store on Main Street and turned it into the Treasury. Now they had a place where they could share their collection with the world. It was also a community space where locals came to gossip and share tales. Business had dwindled as the years went on, but the Rosens weren't going anywhere. You could always count on them for a friendly catch-up.

"Look at you, Rube," Herb said. "So big! How come you don't go to synagogue anymore?"

Rube didn't have an answer. His family hadn't gone to synagogue since before his mom had passed away. *We're Jewish but not go-to-temple-all-the-time Jewish. Not anymore, at least.* "Oh, um, I lost my yarmulke," Rube joked.

"Ha! You're a comedian. Like your father," Herb said. "Once you find that yarmulke, stop by. You always have a place at the Temple Shalom. *All are welcome.*"

"Rueben!" Elanor exclaimed. Her expression was bright and warm. "Come here and give me a hug, handsome boy." Rube rushed over and gave her a tight, warm squeeze. *Feels like home.* "Is your mother with you? I haven't seen her in ages."

Herb put his hand on Elanor's shoulder. "Sweetheart . . ." he said softly.

Elanor loosened her grip and looked disoriented for a moment. "Oh!" she gasped. "I-I-I'm sorry. I thought . . ." She trailed off, afraid to finish her thought.

"Her memory isn't as great as it used to be, Rube," said Herb. "Please forgive her."

Rube understood. *Sort of.* "Don't worry about it." He flashed a kind smile at Elanor to let her know everything was okay. "Mom is always here with us in spirit."

"Look around!" exclaimed Herb. He was desperate to change the subject. "We have a few new items here and there that might tickle your fancy. As always, take your time." Herb motioned to a large wooden cabinet at the front of the store. "That right there is

double-sided. Used to belong to a magician or some such."

Rube opened its doors and looked inside. It was a beautiful piece, but there was no way he'd be able to get it home. *One day, perhaps...*

The Rosens hadn't stocked the place with new items the way they used to. Didn't matter, though. The older stuff was always fun to examine. Rube strolled through the place, checking out all his favorites. There were clocks, lamps, jewelry, kitchen items, furniture, typewriters, coins, drinking glasses, paintings, postcards, mannequins, doorstops, books, pottery, cameras, tin cans, light fixtures, silverware, tools, perfume bottles, and musical instruments. To name a few. A bin of Halloween masks and other holiday paraphernalia sat at the back of the store. Rube was particularly fascinated by an old barber chair in pristine condition. *The magnificence! Too bad I only brought enough money to pay for groceries. Not that I have money anyway. Maybe I need to get a job or something. OoOOooOOoohh, what if I started selling my inventions? I bet I could make at least twenty dollars a piece.*

Then Rube came upon an old music box. *This kind of looks like the one Emilia gave me.* The box had an exotic locking mechanism, and as he activated it, a bell rang and a gust of wind moved through the store. *FWOOSH! No windows open. That's weird.*

As Rube turned down an aisle filled with clocks, he noticed something out of the corner of his eye. A figured was standing nearby, positioned perfectly in the shadows. *Hmmm.* He craned his neck to see if the Rosens were at the checkout counter. *Yep. All accounted for. What now? Am I being followed by a ghost? Should I start screaming and see if it goes away?* He looked down at Bertha, who was cool as a cucumber. *You're no help.* Instead of investigating the would-be specter, Rube dashed around the corner of the aisle and came face-to-face with an unexpected guest.

"Professor Butts!" he shouted. "What are you doing here?!"

"I'm shopping," he deadpanned. "What else would I be doing? Getting my eyebrows waxed? Stay out of my business." The Professor was decked out in a wide-brimmed hat, a long trench coat, and dark glasses. *The town mystery man, living up to his reputation.* The Professor had once been a famous inventor. Now he was a recluse who shunned the spotlight. *Do NOT bother him while his TV shows are on. He hates that.* The internet had told Rube that the Professor was no longer among the living, which didn't make sense, considering they'd interacted in person. *But the internet has been wrong before.* Now here he was, in the flesh, scrutinizing a silver spoon he'd just picked up from a shelf full of dusty cutlery. "This looks nice. Maybe I'll buy it. Unless they have an antique electric toaster lying around. Been hoping to get my hands on one of those for years," he said with a wink.

Does . . . he . . . know???

Rube was puzzled by the Professor's sudden appearance and peculiar behavior. "I didn't think you ventured out of your Haunted Hideaway—" *Don't call it that, dummy.* "I, uh, mean your, um, house."

"Yes, well, you convinced me that perhaps I should interact with the modern world just a bit more. Get the lay of the land. That sort of thing. *For research purposes.*"

"How's that working out for you?"

"It's frightening! How do you stand everything, what with driverless cars and digital assistants and beeping and books on tablets and honking and internet-y poppycock?! Everyone is hunched over looking at their phones, and the only people who benefit are chiropractors! You think the world has been made simpler with all your devices. No, no, no. It's decidedly more complex. *And confusing.*"

"Yeah, it's a lot. But that doesn't mean it's all bad. Unless someone makes a meme of you. That's not always as cool as it sounds."

"What's the matter, Rube? Too famous for your own good? I can imagine being the town hero must be *very stressful*." The Professor chuckled. "That's what you get for being *bold*." *Is he joking right now?!* "Oh, please. Just because I don't own a computer doesn't mean I don't read the paper. Print may be dying but it's not dead yet! What was it like unmasking a dastardly villain for all to see? Did it make you feel empowered?"

"Look, I didn't know Mr. Blank was secretly Professor Zeero, okay? After everyone's machines got all gooped up at Con-Con, I just wanted to build something that made people laugh. How was I supposed to know it'd end up revealing—"

"The oblivious hero," the Professor scoffed, cutting him off. "He knows not how he saves!" *What is he talking about?* "This machine that did the unmasking. What was it called?"

"The Wig Flipper."

"Yes. The Wig Flipper. A clever name, but based on the photographs I saw, the design was terribly lacking, and the construction was . . ." He stroked his chin, trying to come up with the right word. "*Messy*. Yes, that's it. *Messy*. I suppose I was looking for a little bit more *oomph*. A touch of *pizzazz*. Where was your inspiration, boy? Back when I traveled the world, every experience sparked a cacophony of audacious concepts! For instance, when I went over Niagara Falls in a collapsible ash can, I couldn't stop thinking about a simple way to take your own picture. This was before *selfies*. And once, on a jungle expedition, I lay down on a beautiful fur rug that turned out to be a sleeping lion. Who knew! But it gave me an idea for a way to fish an olive out of a long-necked bottle, so that was nice."

Rube's eyes widened in annoyance. He couldn't stand another second of the Professor's droning. "You should be thanking me right now. I took down *your* archenemy!" he said. "You had years to do it and I did it in *one day*. Or actually, a few weeks, I guess, if you want to get technical. Professor Zeero is in jail because of my machine, and *that's a fact*."

"Be careful, boy. Are you sure you want to poke the beast? He might poke back."

The Professor loved conflict and Rube knew it. *"Bring it on."*

"Heh. The fire! I love to see it." The Professor was amused by Rube's intensity. He'd gotten the exact reaction he'd wanted. "This was nice. You seem to have your head together as much as a prepubescent boy can. *Good for you*. At any rate, thank you for continuing not to bother me at home. Good day!"

Ask him. What have you got to lose? He already thinks you're annoying.

"Do you want to chaperone my school dance?!"

That was definitely not the question you had on deck.

"No! Are you out of your gourd?!"

"Sorry. I meant to say, why don't you come over for dinner sometime? Or a snack? Or something. To get out of the house. Move those legs, etcetera."

"*Why don't I come over for dinner sometime?* Well, for starters, I've never been invited . . ."

Rube was testy again. "I'm inviting you now! Can you come over for dinner sometime?"

"I'm sure I *can*. Anyone *can* do *anything* if they put their mind to it," the Professor said, adjusting his dark glasses. "The question is, *will* I?

"All right, never mind. Invitation rescinded! Stay a lonely old creeper. At least you're good at it. Go back to your haunted house and never leave for all I care."

Rube's heightened emotional state entertained the Professor to no end. "To be young and fierce! Oh, the things you could accomplish if you pointed that passion in the right direction!" As the Professor cackled wildly, Rube noticed something bizarre. Bertha, usually an excitable sort, was completely at ease. No barking. No growling. No nothing. She just sat on the floor, panting and staring at an old velvet painting of a wolf. Her docile demeanor caught the Professor's eye. "She's a good girl, isn't she?" he remarked. "How old?"

Rube shrugged. "Don't know exactly. We got her from a shelter. She's a mutt."

"Oh no, no, no." The Professor wagged his finger. "That's a purebred Siberian Cheese Hound right there. A *very* unique breed. I used to have two of them myself. Brie and Manchego. Almost ate me out of house and home, but that's another story."

Rube had stopped messing around. There was serious business that required handling, and he didn't have any more time for small talk. "You mentioned an antique toaster earlier. Why?"

"I've always dreamed of owning an antique electric toaster from the 1920s. Model number one-seventy-seven. Made by the Estate Stove Company in Hamilton, Ohio. *In perfect condition.* The thing makes four slices of toast. Can you imagine? FOUR. SLICES. OF TOAST."

That's what I said. Those are my words. He's talking about my toaster.

FWOOSH! Suddenly the door of the Treasury swung open and an angry man stormed inside. He went straight for the counter where Herb and Elanor were calmly stocking figurines. "Time's up!" the man shouted. Elanor was so startled, she almost dropped a small porcelain doll. "What's the verdict?"

Next to Rube at the back of the store, Bertha immediately

moved into a defensive position. "Hold up, girl," Rube told her. "Let's see what this is about first."

Herb was so nervous, he didn't know what to do with himself. "We need more time to consider your offer, sir," he told the man. "This store is our livelihood. It means everything to us. We can't just sell it off for pennies."

"This place? *A junk store?* It's worth *nothing*." The man sneered. "Look around you. Everyone else is gone. There's nothing left. This town is *done*. You're lucky the Null Corporation offered what they did when they could've just bulldozed this lot and been done with it. Don't be stupid here."

The Null Corporation. That's the company that's buying everything up.

"Please, just tell the town council we need more time," Herb begged.

The man gnashed his teeth in anger. "I *am* the town council. And what *I* say goes. Now, where's that contract?"

As Herb and Elanor scrambled to find the paperwork, Rube and the Professor stewed quietly in the back of the store. "We have to do something," Rube said. "That guy can't just come in here and threaten the Rosens like that. It's not right."

The Professor craned his neck in every direction, looking for machine parts. "I spy a mannequin, some Halloween gear, and a pair of cymbals. All we'd need are a couple more items to create a magnum opus that'll drive that nasty gentleman away from this place for good. Shall we team up?"

"Y-y-you want to team up with m-m-me?" Rube's voice cracked. "T-t-to make a machine?" Anxiety bubbles began stirring inside his stomach. *Keep it together, Goldberg. This is too important to mess up.*

"Oh, quit dithering! Get yourself together, Rube." The Professor pointed to the double-sided cabinet at the front of the store. "That's the key to everything. Help me gather the parts and keep your mouth shut. We don't have much time."

Rube did as he was told. *I get to build a machine with the master machine-maker!* He and the Professor stealthily began grabbing components, mixing and matching bits and pieces as they went. But time was running out. *This is crazy, this is crazy, this is crazy.* A dry run was out of the question. Once they hit upon a workable contraption, it was off to the races. They crept up to the front of the store, hiding behind things so as not to tip off the intruder, who was running his mouth so loudly, he wouldn't have noticed them anyway. *We're doing this. We're actually doing this!* They removed the back of the double-sided cabinet and delicately set up their machine inside. The Professor looked at Rube and nodded. The time had come to cause a little ruckus.

CLANGGG! CLANGGG! CLANGGG!

The cabinet doors flew open as their freakish mannequin machine came to life. It lunged toward the angry man, scaring him half to death. "Son of a . . . !" He attempted to bat the thing away but instead slipped on the floor and fell into a display of old sleigh

bells, which produced a loud and jarring sound. Embarrassed by the episode, the man stood up, adjusted himself, and stared down the Rosens. "*You people* make me sick," he growled. "This isn't over." He stormed out of the store, leaving Herb and Elanor breathless but relieved.

Rube poked his head out from behind the double-sided cabinet. "Everyone safe?"

Herb's hands were shaking. "They want to push us out. They come here and threaten us, call us names. But *we're not budging.*" He slammed his fist onto the counter. "Never again!"

Elanor put her arms around Herb to calm him. "We're safe, my love," she whispered. "Thank you, Rube. That was some quick thinking."

"I couldn't have done it without a little help." Rube turned back to find the Professor had vanished completely. In his place was Bertha, contentedly wagging her tail. "Where'd he go?"

"Who, dear?" Elanor asked. "All I see is a sweet little puppy. Would you like a treat, girl? I bet you would, wouldn't you?"

As she fished a small chewy morsel out of a mason jar on the counter, Rube was left feeling more than a little confused. Had the Professor slipped out the back door to avoid any drama? *He must've. That's the only answer . . . right?* He brushed his concerns about the Professor aside and turned his attention back to Herb and Elanor. "That guy sure had a stick up his butt." *Understatement of the year, Goldberg.*

"The town council thinks it can bully us," Herb said, getting worked up again. "They can send their threatening letters and their goon squad as much as they want! We've been fighting injustice and bigotry our whole lives. And we're not stopping now!"

Elanor smiled brightly, staring at Herb as she hung on his arm. She was enchanted by his fighting spirit. "Can't stop, won't stop!" she declared.

It pleased Rube to see the Rosens bounce back so easily from such a hateful and upsetting episode. But it left him feeling distressed. *Nothing makes sense. First Professor Butts appears, then disappears, and an angry man threatens the sweetest old couple in existence. What the frack is happening around here?!* His anxiety bubbles wouldn't let up.

"Stay for a cup of tea, dear?" Elanor asked.

"I . . . uh . . . no, thanks . . ." Rube waffled. His nerves were fraying. "Bye, now!" Overwhelmed in the moment, he rushed out of the store with Bertha in tow and headed to the grocery store to complete Grandma Etta's errand.

Something in this town is very wrong.

CHAPTER 7

Rube felt nauseated. His stomach did cartwheels the entire way home. As he pedaled faster and faster, he kept thinking about the town councilman screaming at the Rosens. It reminded him of the way Pearl's neighbor had yelled at Isaiah. *That anger.* There had been something vicious in their demeanor that made Rube frightened and furious. Their words echoed in his brain. *You people.* Rube wasn't naïve about racism and bigotry, but he'd never seen it so up close and personal. *I didn't think Beechwood was like that.* There was a rage boiling inside him that made his body tense.

After putting Grandma Etta's groceries away, Rube paced around the house, fidgeting with things in every room. *I gotta get rid of this feeling.* He rearranged two closets, dusted all the banisters, and sorted boxes of miscellaneous machine parts by size *and* color. *I'd clean the toilets too, but only if you paid me.* All that physical activity, but he was still jittery and on edge, stewing in his mind juices. Bertha didn't like that. Her keen senses told her

something was amiss, so she followed him through the house, whimpering and nuzzling at his leg. Rube was too distracted to pay attention until a familiar noise jogged him out of his stupor.

BING BANG BONG. BING BANG BONG.

A video call was coming in from Rube's laptop. He raced through the house to the living room and answered it promptly.

"Hey, buddy!" exclaimed Max. "Long time no see. How's it going?"

"Not well, Dad. Not well at all," Rube growled. "You lied to me."

Yikes, Goldberg. That's the line you choose to open with?

"Whoa, whoa, whoa. Let's start over. I owe you an apology and I know that. I've been completely slammed this week, which is one of the reasons I had to stay in Phoenix longer than I expected. *So many meetings.* You have no idea." Max took a deep breath. "I'm sorry I didn't have the chance to tell you I wasn't coming home when you expected. That's on me."

"It really stunk that I had to hear the news from Oberon."

"Ugh, that stupid bird!" Max exclaimed. He and Oberon weren't on squawking terms. "Grandma Etta needs to control that thing or we're having it for Thanksgiving."

"Thanks for the antique toaster, by the way. Even though it doesn't make up for—"

"Antique toaster?"

"Yeah. You sent me an antique toaster. From Phoenix. To smooth over your lies . . ."

"Enough with the lies thing. *I* didn't send you a toaster. Did you order something online to get back at me? Rube, I swear, if I see some random charge on my credit card, you're going to be in big trouble . . ."

If he didn't send it, who did? GASP. *It must have been Professor Butts! But wait a minute. He said he wanted one for himself, so why would he send one to me? Let it go, Goldberg. Don't waste this time with Dad.*

"JK! All good. Just havin' a li'l fun with you, Pop. Hehe."

Max wasn't exactly buying Rube's line, but he didn't have the time or energy to inquire further. "What did you get up to today? Besides school. You're still going to school, right? Please tell me you're still going to school."

Rube anxiously twiddled his fingers. "School is school. Homework sucks. There's a dance I don't want to go to. And Pearl is running for class president." *Say the thing that's bursting to free itself from your brain.* "But there's something else I need to talk about. Something serious. I stopped by the Treasury on my way to pick up groceries for Grandma Etta, and a weird thing happened."

"You know Herb and Elanor are getting older. Not as sharp as they used to be. It happens. Did Elanor call you Ron? She does that sometimes."

Tell him. Tell him everything. Do it now.

"No, it wasn't that. A guy from the town council threatened them. I saw the whole thing. He called them 'you people,' and after he left, Herb got super mad and said, 'Never again.'"

"Hoo boy," Max said, shaking his head in dismay. "That's really upsetting to hear. *Really upsetting.* Are they okay? Are *you* okay? No one got hurt, right?"

"I'm fine. The Rosens are too, I guess. But . . ." *Just say it, Rube. Admit how you felt.* "The guy was *really* mad. It was scary."

Max sighed. "Yeah. I bet it was. This town has a lot of work to do."

"What does that mean?"

"Rube," Max said, running his fingers through what little was left of his hair all the way down to the back of his neck, which he began to massage. "These are conversations we should have face-to-face."

"You're always gone, though," replied Rube. *Ouch. But true.*

"Yeah, okay, so . . ." Max paused to collect his thoughts. "There are things you don't know about Beechwood. Stuff they don't teach you in school. Historical stuff. Long story short, this town has had some major problems over the years, and no matter how much we think it's changed, sometimes bad people rear their ugly heads and remind us there's always work to be done."

"If Beechwood is bad, then why are *we* here?"

"I didn't say Beechwood was *bad*." Now Max was getting frustrated. "First of all, there's bad stuff *everywhere*. Even in places people think are good. That's why you have to call out injustice, *fight it*, and keep fighting. Let me tell you a little story. Before you were born, your mom and I moved to a new town. On the outside it looked nice. Lots of trees. Everything was clean. But some of the people in town pretended to be something they weren't."

"Double agents for a top-secret government agency?"

"No, I mean they were bigots. They didn't like that we were Jewish. Our neighbors would smile at us, make small talk, and then talk smack about us behind our backs. That, and leave crude spray-painted messages in our yard. Most of the time when we faced bigots and racists, they were screaming, angry, and easy to identify. But it's the quiet ones you have to watch out for. Anyway, we'd saved up a long time to buy our dream home, and we weren't going to give it up just because a bunch of ignorant people wanted us to leave."

"So, what did you do?"

"First I have to tell you what we *didn't* do. This is extremely embarrassing, but it's the truth and you deserve to know it. One

131

night, in a fit of anger, I told your mom that we should change our last name to something less Jewish-sounding. Like Smith or, I don't know, George. Then people wouldn't give us such a hard time and we could live in peace. Boy, did she blow a fuse at me for suggesting that. 'This is your family name, Maxwell! Your parents didn't escape the Nazis so you could become someone else! We're not changing a darn thing!' Except she didn't say *darn*. And she had a good point. I was ashamed to have even suggested it, but I was young and desperate to fit in."

"I would've been Rube George, the boy with two first names. Doesn't have a catchy ring to it, so thanks for avoiding that mistake. What happened next?"

"We stayed, with the intention of working our butts off and making the town better. We got involved. We spoke with our neighbors. We started committees and councils. Pearl's parents, Marcus and Monica, felt the same way we did, and together we helped build a better community. Things changed because we made them change. Everyone felt it. New families moved to town, and we became the welcoming and inclusive neighborhood we wanted to be."

"Wait. This bigoted town you were talking about was *Beechwood*?!"

"Yep."

"But I don't get it. If the town *changed,* then why is bigotry still happening?"

Max wiped the sweat from his forehead. "I was not expecting to have this conversation until you were much older, never mind *tonight*, but we're *here,* so let's keep the ball rolling." He gulped. "Bigotry and racism are baked into a lot of stuff. They're like machines, actually. There are lots of different parts, and when they all work together, the results are very harmful. *Really* terrible. And these machines have been around for a long time. They're part of history, sadly. But the good news is that these machines can be disassembled. Brave people have been taking them apart, piece by piece, with activism and education. Others just smash the machines. I say do whatever works. The key, though, is understanding how these machines operate so they can never be assembled again."

Now you're talkin' my language. "My teachers never said anything about racist machines in elementary school. Why didn't they teach me this stuff?"

"Some adults like to roll the bad stuff out over time. That way you're not overwhelmed as a seven-year-old. Though I suppose if you can handle the tooth fairy not being real, you can understand systems of oppression."

"What are systems of oppression?"

"It's when laws and rules are made that treat certain groups of people unequally and unfairly in our society."

"Why would anyone want to do that?"

Max sighed. "I've asked myself that very question. I'm afraid the answer is upsetting. You see, Rube, the cruelty is the point. These people want others to suffer. It makes them feel powerful. They'll say it's just a simple matter of disagreement, but it's not. Trust me. I've confronted plenty of grinning bigots in my day. They come in all shapes and sizes. The truth was best summed up by a writer named Robert Jones Jr., who said, 'We can disagree and still love each other unless your disagreement is rooted in my oppression and denial of my humanity and right to exist.'"

Max could see the confusion on his son's face. "It means we can disagree on stuff like movies and baseball, but if you vote for and support people who want to make others suffer and take away their basic rights? Then we have a real problem."

"So you knew about this all along? When were you going to tell me?!"

"When the time was right. Which, I guess, is tonight. Look, Rube, the world can be terrible sometimes, and I want to protect you from that. All parents want to protect their kids from the terribleness, but it's not . . ." Max scrunched his face into a ball. "It's not truthful to do that. Everything is not all right. Our country doesn't treat all its people equally, and that needs to change."

"When you say 'its people,' do you mean Native Americans? Because I already know about that and it's messed up."

"God, your mom would have been *so much* better at this. Let me put it this way: American history is more complex than what you read in your textbooks. Sometimes those books are written by bad people who only want to make themselves look good. They don't want to explain the ugly truths."

"If America is bad, then why did our Jewish ancestors come here?"

"It's not . . ." Max bit his lip and cracked his knuckles. "You're *really* making me work here, Rube. I wasn't prepared to give you a rundown of American history *tonight*."

"Yeah, but it's the truth. If you don't tell the truth, then you're lying."

Max sighed. "You're absolutely right." He rubbed his chin and thought out loud. "How about this? There are shelves of history books in my study that we can read and discuss once I get back home. Like our own little book club. How does that sound?"

"Pearl and her parents do that." Rube shook his head in disbelief. "But if she's been learning about this stuff all along, why hasn't she told *me*?"

"It's not her job to educate you. It's *mine*. It's your school's. It's the responsibility of our community at large. What's funny is that I'd planned on talking to you about all of this at some point in the near future, but then . . ."

"You got busy."

"Yes. Which is not a good excuse, I know." Max moved closer to the camera and spoke from a place deep within his heart. "Rube, I'm doing the best I can here. Losing your mom was the start of a very tough time for this family. If *I* don't work, *you* don't eat. I want to be with you right now more than anything on the planet. You know that. Please just try to understand where I'm coming from. That's all I ask. Listen, when I get home, we'll spend some time in my library and do all kinds of reading. *Together*. I promise. Deal?"

"Deal."

"Right on." Max leaned back in his chair, relieved. "I love you, Rube. More than you'll ever know. It makes me happy that you're so interested in these things. It's the right way to be. You make this world better by being in it, and I'm proud of you."

There were still questions nagging at the back of Rube's mind. "I know some people don't like Jews, but no one has ever said anything mean to *me*."

"They don't have to. Hate can be silent. That's why you keep your eyes open and call it out when you see it. Stand up for people. And stand *against* bullies and bigots. History was yesterday, son. Just because you don't see the bad stuff doesn't mean it's not out there. But here's another thing you need to understand, so listen up. There's good stuff too. *Lots of it.* Everywhere you look! Hold on to that, okay? Don't get discouraged. I know how that obsessive little brain of yours works. I don't want you stressing out about this."

I'm already stressed out about it. And I miss Mom again.

"I'm going to do some studying now, I think."

"Good boy. Putting schoolwork first. That's what I'm talking about."

Technically not what I was talking about. But I'll let you think that.

Max beamed. "I love you. And I'm grateful for you."

"Love you too," Rube replied.

After the call ended, Rube sat down on the couch. *What an*

info dump that was. He was in a daze. Bertha noticed and hopped up on his lap to keep him company. *I have to do something.* Rube felt hollow and helpless. He wanted answers. He needed solutions. *Now.* And he wasn't going to wait for Max to get home to find some. *And so it begins.*

He went into his dad's office to have himself a little browse. *Hmmm. What do we have here?* Most of the books in Max's library were meant for a much older audience. But that didn't matter much to Rube. *I'll figure it out as I go.* There were books on race, religion, and history. Some were serious while others had a humorous flair. *One time Dad referred to some of these authors as "great thinkers," but I can't remember their names.* Now, confronted with hundreds of books staring back at him, Rube was in a quandary as to which direction to take. He spotted a title that caught his eye and removed it from the shelf. *Little Man, Little Man: A Story of Childhood* by James Baldwin.

"This looks like a good place to start . . ."

CHAPTER 8

"Look, Mom!" Rube shouted from atop the jungle gym.

Hannah, Rube's mother, had been watching him on the playground for hours. She never tired of seeing him happy and active. "My little monkey boy!" she exclaimed. "Show me what you got!" Little Rube swung himself across the monkey bars, his arms barely able to reach from one bar to the next. "C'mon, buddy! You're almost there."

His journey nearing completion, Rube reached for the final bar, but his fingers slipped, and he fell to the ground with force. *Oh no.* He lay there quietly and looked up at the sky. *I'm a failure.* The angry voices inside his head grew louder and louder. *You couldn't do it, could you? You can't do anything.*

"Shhhh! Rube, don't listen to them," Hannah commanded. "I believe in you."

How did she know?

Her words were music to Rube's ears. They flowed through him like fuel, energizing his body from his fingertips to his toes. *You can do this. You can do this.* He launched himself up from the ground and got back on the jungle gym lickety-split.

"That's the spirit!" Hannah cheered.

This time, Rube focused his attention on the final bar. It didn't matter how long it took or what happened in between; getting to that bar was the goal, and he wouldn't take his eyes off the prize. Rube reached out his arm and began his journey. Slowly, he swung from one bar to the next, never losing sight of his target. *Three more bars. Two more. One more bar!*

Hannah could barely contain her glee. "Almost there!"

Rube reached out, grabbed the final bar, and swung himself onto it. "I did it!"

Hannah raced over, swept her son into her arms, and gave him a big hug. "You did it! I'm so proud of you!" She whisked him off of the jungle gym and through the air, twirling him in every direction. Rube giggled with happiness until Hannah planted him back on the ground and gazed deep into his eyes. "Did you find it?" she asked.

Rube didn't understand the question. "Did I find what?"

"Did you find what I left for you?" replied Hannah. "I need to know that you found what I left for you, Rube. Tell me you found what I left for you."

Without warning, Lala appeared at the top of the slide. "Nous triompherons. Nous prévaudrons. Ensemble!" she exclaimed. "Comprenez-vous?"[1]

What is happening!?

Rube turned back around to find his mother had gone. "Mom? Mom!" he cried. But Hannah was nowhere to be found. She was gone without a trace. As the skies darkened, Rube became nervous. Anxiety bubbles began growling deep within his stomach.

1   French translation: "We will triumph. We will prevail. Together! Do you understand?"

"You're not supposed to be here," Zach said, poking his head out from behind a tree. *"Or are you?"*

Pearl tapped Rube on the back, startling him. "Are you going to do it?" she asked.

"Do *what?!*" he replied. In the blink of an eye, Rube's classmates invaded the area from all sides like zombies on the attack. He shut his eyes and wished them all away. "Leave me alone!" But nothing happened. As his friends moved closer and closer, a blinding white light flared above Rube. He reached out for it and was instantly whisked away from the madness.

"Gah!" Rube exclaimed. Now he was on the couch, laptop on his chest, surrounded by piles and piles of books. *It was all just a dream. Or nightmare, actually.* Rube sat up and felt a bright warmth on his face. *Sunlight. OMG, it's morning!* He'd fallen asleep in the living room. "This is bad, this is bad, this is bad," he mumbled to himself as he ran upstairs and threw on some fresh clothes. *No time to waste!* He scrambled to school, energized and ready to tell his friends the things he had uncovered during his late-night history lesson.

I know the secret history of Beechwood.

Rube's chat with his father had compelled him to investigate the things they'd spoken about. He started with books for younger readers, but they hadn't given him what he needed. *I want real stuff I can sink my teeth into.* He had browsed his father's library, stacking books in piles that were as tall as he was. *Not quite. I'm taller, thanks.* Once he'd assembled his reading materials, he cuddled up with Bertha on the couch and dove in headfirst. The more he had discovered, the more curious it made him. One thing had led to another, and soon he was on his computer, cross-referencing. Then came the eBooks. Suddenly, history wasn't as far away as it had once been. He'd been bombarded with hard truths like never before, and they caused Rube to feel disappointed in himself. When he built machines, he always looked deeper. *That's how you make sure something is functioning the right way.* But when it came to history, he hadn't done his due diligence. He'd accepted everything at face value and had now come to learn that was a huge mistake.

Never again.

Rube couldn't get to school fast enough. While he put the pedal to the metal, his friends and classmates mingled in the school courtyard, waiting for that first-period bell to ring. Boob had been waiting patiently near the bike rack by himself, but since Rube was a no-show, he decided to do a little mingling on his own. Reina was camped out under one of the voluminous sycamore trees, and Boob saw an opportunity for a friendly chat.

"Whatcha workin' on?" he asked.

"A thing for science class," she replied. "It's about how hundred-million-year-old microbes under the sea floor were revived by scientists using a little food and oxygen. Bonkers stuff."

"That's kind of like me and cereal. One bowl of Honeybursts and I'm practically a new person!" Boob reached into his pocket and tossed a package of chocolate wafers onto Reina's paper. "A little pick-me-up in case you need it. They're German. Frau Rodriguez gave some to anyone who scored above seventy-five percent on the pop quiz, but *I* got them from Justin Chung, since he's better at pop quizzes than I am."

"Thanks, I guess?" Reina said, slipping the wafers into her backpack.

Boob lingered awkwardly. "Are you a member of the Pride Alliance?"

"Why do you ask?"

"Oh, um . . . I just thought . . ." Boob waffled. "Is it fun?"

Reina smiled. "Yeah, it's cool. One of the better clubs at this school. Boring sometimes, but we've had a couple great outings. No one wants to go to a metal show, though, which is stupid. You into ethical taxidermy?"

"Uhhhh, I don't know what that is . . ."

"Yeah, neither does anyone in the Pride Alliance. That's why I'm trying to get them to do a roadkill scoop one of these days. As a team-building exercise or something. My aunt turned me on to taxidermy when we visited her a couple of years ago in Alaska. Are you thinking about going?"

"To Alaska? I mean, sure. It seems like a *chill* place."

Reina laughed. "No, I mean the Pride Alliance meetings."

"Me? Well, uh, I don't . . ." Before Boob had a chance to answer, Rube roared into the schoolyard on his bike, kicking up dust as he went.

"STOP EVERYTHING! We need to talk!" he yelled.

Before Boob and Reina could ask Rube what he was so worked up about, Pearl stormed over to the three of them, a pile of crumpled, ripped-up papers in her hand.

"Someone tore down all my flyers!" she exclaimed.

"The ones *we* made?" Reina asked. Pearl nodded.

Boob was flummoxed. "The ones *you* made. As in, *both of you?*"

"Reina is helping me run my campaign," replied Pearl. "She's smart, clever, and thorough. And she makes a tight French bread pizza. That cool with you?"

"Yeah! Why wouldn't it be? Reina is great." Boob was inexplicably flustered. "She should run everything! If she wants to. Don't listen to me! I just ate candy for breakfast. You were saying?"

"Look at *this*." Pearl held up a canvas tote with Emilia Harris's face on it that said PICK ME in big letters. "Emilia is running for president too and has been passing out gift bags filled with expensive stuff to anyone who asks. And apparently her rich parents are hiring a skywriter to draw her face in clouds above the school."

"That's not right," Rube growled.

"Emilia's mom is a famous yoga lady, and her dad is a city official. They can pretty much do whatever they want." Pearl threw her hands up. "How am I supposed to compete with that kind of money?!"

The group went silent for a minute as they brainstormed ways to counteract Emilia's public relations assault.

"Hmmm. Emilia has a huge following. What if you did crazy wild things on your social media? You'd get lots of attention!" Boob exclaimed. "Maybe not the good kind, though."

"*No.* We've been through this," Pearl said firmly. "That stuff is just a distraction. The *posting* and the *checking*, the posting and the checking . . . it's all too much. I'm too busy. And *likes* don't translate to *votes.*"

"What if they *could?* What if I made a machine that helped promote your candidacy?" Rube suggested. "Something that raised awareness. We could call it the Elevate-Or!"

Pearl winced at the thought. "Thanks for the suggestion, Rube, but what I need is *tangible* help. A machine is fine and everything, but I really need people to spread the word. I need them to show up for me."

"Understood!" Rube said. "I promise to do whatever it takes to help you get elected. But first there's something I have to tell you. *All of you.* About Beechwood."

"Wait a minute!" exclaimed Boob, eyeing Rube suspiciously. "Red eyes. Messy hair. Sniff, sniff—*stank* breath. You were up all night building stuff, weren't you?"

"No, I was . . ." Rube's heart rate quickened. His anxiety bubbles were bubbling. It felt like his throat was strangling itself. *This is not good.* Pearl saw the impending panic attack and reminded Rube to relax.

"*Breathe*, Rube," she said. Her voice was calm and soothing. "What's going on?"

"I stayed up late last night reading history books—"

"Yuck!" Boob shrieked. "School?! *At night?!* What's wrong with you?" Rube's icy glare told him this wasn't a time for joking around. "Sorry. *Go on.*"

"Lately I've been noticing things I haven't seen before. Like the way people act and stuff. It started with Pearl's neighbor. She was nasty toward Isaiah, and he hadn't even done anything wrong."

"Well, she's racist," said Pearl. "That's what she does."

"Yeah, but it didn't make sense to me. Then yesterday I was at the Treasury, and a man came in, *a town council person*, and started yelling at the Rosens, trying to bully them out of their business. There was something familiar in his tone that reminded me of your hateful neighbor. So I talked to my dad about it, and he said there's history we don't know about. Stuff they don't even teach us."

Boob didn't understand. "What does history have to do with Pearl's racist neighbor?"

"I'm about to tell you!" Rube calmed himself and continued. "Last night I read a bunch of books from my dad's library. Well, some of them I skimmed, but I read *a lot,* and let me tell you, we're not getting the full story around here. Beechwood used to be a sundown town."

Boob poked Rube with his elbow. "Sounds like an old Western movie. Oooo! Or a fancy resort."

"Yeah, if fancy resorts were all about discrimination," Reina chimed in. "From the 1930s through the 1960s, sundown towns were all-white communities built to be segregated. They wrote the laws a certain way so Black people, Jewish people, and other non-white people couldn't live there. There were a bunch of them all over the United States. Still are if you look hard enough."

"Is that true?" asked Boob. "That can't be true."

"It's one hundred percent true," Rube replied. "Black people weren't allowed within the Beechwood city limits after dark, and if they got caught, the town's people would hurt them. Back then, Black people had to make their own travel guide about how to avoid racist towns. It was crazy!"

"I don't want to live here anymore," Boob said, crossing his arms. "I'm not living in some nasty old racist town!"

Pearl snickered. "Where are you going to go to escape racism? Beechwood wasn't the *only* sundown town in America. There were lots of them. Moving away from the problem isn't going to solve it. What you're supposed to do is stay and fight."

"The lady has a point," said Reina.

"She always does," Rube replied.

"Fine. So what do we do?" asked Boob.

"We take down white supremacy, smash the patriarchy, and protect our LGBTQ+ brothers and sisters!" Rube shouted so loud, he attracted the attention of other students in the vicinity. "Sorry. I'm really keyed up right now."

"What time are we doing all this?" asked Boob. "My sister is taking me to see the new *Commander Long Johns* movie tonight. In this one he actually *wears pants*."

"Cut it out with the jokes, Boob. This is serious, and we have to face it. *Head-on.* James Baldwin once said, 'Not everything that is faced can be changed, but nothing can be changed until it is faced.'"

"You're quoting Baldwin now?" asked Pearl.

"He's one of the most important Black American voices of the twenty-first century!"

"Yes, he is. I just didn't know *you* knew that."

Rube, you dummy. You're not listening to yourself. "I'm so, *so* sorry. I'm supposed to say African American and not Black, right? Aw, man, I'm messing everything up already."

Pearl saw Rube getting worked up and put her hand on his shoulder to calm him down. "We're friends, Rube. I know who you are, and as *messy* as you can be . . ." *There's that word again.* "I know you mean well. So here's the deal. I'm cool with being called Black. Some people want to be called African American. If you call them Black, they might correct you. Take the note and move on. No big deal."

"Same goes for pronouns," Reina added. "Just ask nicely if you don't know. It's really not *that* big of a deal as long as you're not rude about it."

"Understood," Rube said.

"Superintendent Atwater def knows about the whole sundown thing," said Reina. "His family has been a part of this town's inner workings for generations." *That's right! I saw that somewhere in my research.* "The guy's name is in our history textbooks!" *What?! I missed that tidbit.* "There has to be a connection."

"Let's see . . ." Rube got one of his dad's history books out of his backpack, eager to share another of his discoveries. As he flipped through its pages, a note fell out. *What is this?* It was a checklist written on lined paper. *In my mom's handwriting.* Though the ink had faded and the note was worn, the text was as clear as day.

LISTEN MORE.

EDUCATE YOURSELF.

SPEAK OUT!

USE YOUR VOICE TO LIFT OTHERS.

STAND UP FOR THE PEOPLE WHO NEED YOU AND STAY STANDING. DO THE WORK!

A note from my mom to . . . herself . . . or . . . to me? As Rube stared at the crinkly piece of paper, a lump grew in his throat. *I miss her so much.*

BRRRRRRRRING!

The bell rang to signal it was time for class. Rube stuffed the paper back into the book and put them both in his backpack. "I've got another idea."

Boob had seen that look on Rube's face before. "Oh, he's feelin' feisty now. What are you gonna do? Storm into the principal's office and *demand justice?*"

"Something like that." Rube swung his backpack over his shoulder and marched toward the building. "Feel free to join me if you want! The more the merrier."

"I was just kidding!" Boob shouted. "Should we join him? I'm not dressed for justice."

Reina was impressed. "Didn't expect such a hasty response from that one. I'm definitely here for it."

"When Rube gets something in his head, it becomes hard to dislodge," said Pearl. "We better go with him in case his mouth writes a check his butt can't cash."

"Butts cashing checks?! Butts who are also professors?! What is this world coming to?!" Boob said frantically.

Rube marched through the hallways of Beechwood Middle feeling empowered and ready to fight. *Not actually fight, like with fists and stuff. Like . . . fight the power. You know what I mean.* The first hurdle was getting past Principal Kim's assistant, Miss Mary. *We have history.* She was as sweet as could be, but as a highly trained former member of the military, nothing escaped her sight. Miss Mary was the perfect person for vice principal and had campaigned for the position over the summer, but pesky "budget cuts" had eliminated the role entirely. *I'm surprised she stuck around.* Upon arriving at the front office, Rube and his friends peered through the doorway to find Miss Mary talking on the phone and looking profoundly worried. *Something is wrong.*

"It's getting worse," she said in a hushed voice. "All these changes, and I still don't think we'll be able to save it. Oh, yes, Atwater is the worst. Horrible. A real *ass*. But what can I do? He runs everything. I just worry about the students. If they only knew . . ."

"First thing in the morning and Miss Mary is already stressed out?" whispered Boob. "Maybe this isn't the right time."

"It's never going to be the right time. That's why we just have to do it," Rube said, forging ahead. "Hey, Miss Mary! We're here to see Superintendent Atwater. We know he's in there. His ugly yellow car is parked outside." Instead of stopping and waiting for Miss Mary's approval to enter, like he had originally planned to do, Rube just kept walking. He swung open the door and went straight into Principal Kim's office. *Feels like the right thing at the right time.* "Morning!" he said in a chipper voice. "How's everyone feeling today?"

Principal Kim was sitting with Superintendent Atwater, going over a stack of very important-looking papers. "Rube!" he said, startled. "What are you doing?"

Good question. I'm not entirely sure of the answer. Maybe I should have thought this through a bit more. The moment had overwhelmed Rube's senses. He didn't quite have the words. *Yet.* What he did have were friends gathered in the doorway behind him as backup.

Principal Kim was starting to get steamed. "Rube, you can't just barge in here and do whatever you want at any given time! That's not how things work."

Say something. Do something. Anything, Golberg. Rube fished his history textbook out of his backpack and

tossed it onto Superintendent Atwater's lap. *Which he did not like.* "Why don't our history textbooks tell the truth about this town? Or the country, for that matter? *You're* not a historian, but for some reason you're listed as an author. What's up with *that?*"

Atwater's hands shook with anger as he placed the textbook on the desk. "I've written quite a few published texts. Power affords one opportunity, and the truth is . . . let's just say . . . subjective. Not that your brain is capable of understanding something so complex." *Rude.* "This school didn't have the funds to buy new materials, which was a terrible shame. So I kindly donated these and bestowed the gift of knowledge upon the student body, choosing to focus on the positive parts of history."

"It's not the *truth,*" Rube pressed.

"If you want to know more, there are plenty of other books in the library downtown. Now, remove yourselves from this room or face expulsion."

"You lied," Rube shot back, unfazed.

Welp. Guess it doesn't matter now. Expulsion, here I come!

"I did not lie," Atwater growled.

"You *did,* actually," Principal Kim said sheepishly. "*Technically.* Or the book did. A lie of omission is still a lie. And now that I think about it, I really should have read the fine print before I agreed to use it."

Atwater was displeased to hear that. "You'll speak when spoken to, *Ted*." *Ouch*. "As for you children, get to class immediately or . . ."

"We're not going anywhere," Rube declared. "You can't just erase the past and pretend like it didn't happen. This whole town was built on racism. You're from one of Beechwood's founding families, Atwater. You *know* it was a sundown town."

Principal Kim waved his hand through the air. "Wait a minute. Back up. What?!"

"What a sad bit of history you've found." Atwater's smile was as fake as his alligator shoes. "An unfortunate stain on Beechwood's past, and something a child could never understand. But times have changed. The world is a different place now. No need to dwell."

"The world isn't as different as you think," said Rube. "But it will be."

Atwater narrowed his eyes. "If Beechwood is such a horrible place, why are you still here? Why are your families here? Did you ever think of *that*?"

"I had the same question," Rube confessed. "But my friend Pearl here is right. Moving away from the problem isn't going to solve it. What you're supposed to do is stay and fight."

Pearl reached into her pocket, pulled out a PEARL HAS A PLAN button, and pinned it on Superintendent Atwater. "Vote for Pearl," she said, grinning. "For change!"

Atwater glared at Rube. "You read a book and now you know *everything*. Is that it? If I had talked like this to one of my elders when *I* was a young man, I would have received a spanking."

Ew. Gross.

Principal Kim, uncomfortable with the direction the conversation was headed, did his best to deescalate the situation. "Everyone, let's take a step back, cool off, and start over. Okay?"

All right. I think I can do that. Rube considered his words and softened his tactics. "'We can disagree and still love each other. Unless your disagreement is rooted in my oppression and denial of my humanity and right to exist.' Robert Jones Jr. said that. You should check out one of his books someday. You might learn something."

"Ha," Atwater scoffed. "You're far too young to be reading books you don't understand."

"Women didn't have the right to vote until 1920, interracial marriage wasn't legal until 1967, and LGBTQ+ people couldn't be out and proud in the military until 2010. Those are just a few of the things I learned by reading. And I understand all of *that* just fine," Rube replied.

Boob chimed in, "You know, I was thinking . . ." *Uh-oh. Boob is thinking again. This could go a lot of different ways.* "Black history is American history, but we only talk about it in February, during its special month. And this school doesn't teach any LGBTQ+ history *at all.*"

Atwater had reached his limit. The outrage that had been stewing inside him was at a tipping point. The veins on his forehead were bulging. The spray he used to color his hair dripped down his cheek and onto his shirt. *This guy looks like he's about to pop!* "Well, why don't we just teach the history of EVERYTHING, then?!" Atwater bellowed, launching out of his chair in a rage.

"*Dude.* That's exactly what we're saying," Reina deadpanned.

Principal Kim took control of the situation. "Kids, this is terribly out of order, and you should be ashamed of yourselves for causing such a ruckus," he said, winking directly at Rube. *Principal Kim is up to something.* "Here at Beechwood Middle School, we focus on the Five Cs—critical thinking, creativity, communication, collaboration, and character. I haven't seen them displayed in your actions today, and that's disappointing. Therefore, you'll *all* be receiving a reprimand *and* detention. Come with me."

Principal Kim ushered Rube and his friends out of the office, closing the door tightly behind him. "*Phew.* That got intense there for a minute."

"You're on our side, right, Principal Kim?" asked Rube. "You see how Atwater really is, don't you?"

Principal Kim chose his words carefully. "Rube, your behavior was rude and disruptive, but . . ." He paused. "You're right." *I knew it.* "I was hired by the school board to enact their agenda. I didn't know when I signed on that their agenda was bad for students in a lot of different ways. I've done everything I can to stop them, but . . ." He looked at Miss Mary, who was shaking her head. "I've said too much. Please believe that I'm doing everything I can to make this school a better place. We have some big obstacles to overcome, but I'm fighting for you every single day. I suggest you bring these issues to light during the election. Let the students hear what you have to say."

"That's the plan." Pearl grinned.

"We're not really in trouble, are we?" asked Boob. "My dad will freak out if he sees the school's number pop up on his caller ID."

"I'll smooth things over with Atwater, but I *will* have to write you up," Principal Kim said. "A reprimand or something. Don't worry, no one is calling your parents. For now, though, I need all of you to get to class. Go, go, go."

Rube, Boob, Pearl, and Reina scrambled out of the principal's office and down the hallway toward their classrooms. They felt invigorated. And a little scared. Challenging the superintendent had been the right thing to do, but they wondered if their plan might backfire.

"I can't believe we did that," Rube said, breathless. "My heart is racing."

"Honestly, I'm really happy someone stood up to that pig," replied Reina.

"Nice work in there, Rube," Pearl said, beaming. "Didn't think you had it in you." *Me neither.* "But I'm glad to see I was wrong."

"I wish I could just build a machine that would solve the world's problems and make things better."

"You can," Pearl assured him. "Real change just takes a different set of tools."

Real change just takes a different set of tools.
Huh.

CHAPTER 9

The days following Rube's confrontation with Atwater were tense. Despite Principal Kim's assurances, no one felt safe from whatever trouble might await them. *We have to stay vigilant.* With the superintendent's deep and murky connections to Beechwood's sordid history, anything was possible. *What if Atwater sends a team of assassins to knock us off one by one?! Or what if he kidnaps us and throws us in an underground prison where we're forced to shovel coal or, I don't know, fight each other for porridge?! That would be very bad. But unlikely. Right?! Ugh, I really need to relax, don't I?*

So Rube and his friends kept a low profile. They didn't talk, hang out, or interact at school. Rube got the idea from a movie where a bunch of people were targeted by a shadowy secret agency and, in order to avoid capture, they split up and went in their own directions. After school, Rube stayed home with Bertha and spent his free time reading, biking, and—what else—designing machines. There was one contraption in particular that he couldn't wait to show his friends. *Not "friends." Pearl. I can't wait to show Pearl.* Anxious to help Pearl with her campaign, Rube decided to debut his newest creation at school as a way to make up for the disaster at the garden unveiling. *And I think she's gonna love it!* But he was nervous that he might mess things up. *Again.* Needing a little advice on how to be less anxious, Rube did something he'd been meaning to do since school had started. He went to visit Ms. Laffin, the guidance counselor.

Ms. Laffin was a jittery lady—an odd trait for someone who got paid to help calm the nerves of students. Everything scared her. *Everything.* Once, Rube arrived at school early and saw Ms. Laffin accidentally walk into a spiderweb. *She freaked out. Big-time.* Her screams were so loud as she pulled the dewy fibers from her face, the neighborhood cats were traumatized by the sound. Now she walked with an umbrella everywhere she went. Another time, Boob swore he saw her choke on air. *Don't know if I believe that one.* But despite her propensity for panic, Ms. Laffin was a warm and genuine soul whose door was always open to the students of Beechwood. "Knock first!" she always said. And that's exactly what Rube did. But in true Ms. Laffin fashion, she wasn't the least bit ready.

"Yipe!" she screeched. In her surprised state, Ms. Laffin swept her arm through the air, upsetting a steaming thermos of coffee, which cascaded across her desk, drenching all of her papers and soaking her beautiful leather-bound notebook. "Oh, *nuts.*"

"I did knock first," Rube said, chagrined.

Ms. Laffin smiled and nodded. "And I appreciate that! It's been a very long day. Come! Have a seat, Rube. Let's chat."

Rube eyed the messy office, taking in every nook and cranny. "You really need something that can help you clean your workspace. A machine that can file your papers, or mop up spills. I'd be happy to build it. No cost!"

"Thanks, that's quite all right. But thank you!" she said, cleaning up the coffee spill. "What an honor it would be to have an original Rube Goldberg Machine someday. But right *now,* I'd like to focus on *you.* What brings you by?"

Rube sat down, searching for the right words to explain his situation. *Just tell her what's on your mind.* "I've been having strange dreams . . ." *That's not why you're here, but sure, waste this nice lady's time. It's not like she has a million other important things to do.*

"Hmmmm. You know, sometimes anxiety and stress can manifest in dreams. Anxiety and stress can manifest in all kinds of interesting ways, actually." She pointed to Rube's face. "Like that pimple on the tip of your nose."

What pimple on the tip of my nose?! Rube scrambled over to a nearby mirror to assess the damage. *Aw, man, this is the worst.*

"Is there something in particular that's weighing heavily on you?" Ms. Laffin asked. "Talk to me."

Rube plopped back down in his chair and tried to loosen up. "I think about *a lot* of stuff. All the time. It's really hard to turn my brain off. And sometimes I think about stuff so much that I get this feeling . . ."

Ms. Laffin nodded kindly. "How does this feeling *feel?*"

"Like there's a tornado in my stomach. I call them my anxiety bubbles. Sometimes I can't think straight. I start shaking. And I sweat."

"Uh-huh. And what, specifically, causes you to worry like this? Can you tell me?"

Where do I begin? I'm worried about my dad, my friends, my family, my dog, my town, my life. I'm worried that I'm going to fail. I'm worried that my friends are disappointed in me. I want to end racism and bigotry. I want to change hearts and minds! I want to solve problems! I want to build machines that will change the world! I'm worried that I'll never be able to do any of that. It drives me crazy! And I miss my mom.

"This is a safe space, Rube. You can say anything you think or feel."

You came to her office to get stuff off your chest, so get stuff off your chest already.

"I don't know," Rube replied. *Ugh, you're impossible, Goldberg.*

"What I think you need are strong tools to help you manage these 'anxiety bubbles,' but before I go into that, tell me, how do you usually unwind after a long day at school?"

"I sketch and build machines."

"Of course you do! How silly of me to even ask. May I see some of your sketches?"

Rube reached into the back of his pants, pulled out his notebook, and showed Ms. Laffin some of his work. "I design *a lot* of machines. Way more than I can actually build. I have a thing for vintage items, so sometimes I'll sketch machines using them. Other times I'll draw fantasy machines like roller coasters or space stations." He flipped to the back of the notebook. "Lately I've been doodling cartoon characters. Doing little comic strips. I don't know, it's stupid, but I like it."

"It's not stupid at all! It's quite impressive. Creating art is a great stress reliever and can be very therapeutic. But it doesn't mean the things we think about will mysteriously go away on their own. We still have to deal with them. Tell me, do you have a mantra?"

"What is that? An underwater spaceship?"

"A mantra is a positive affirmation. Something you say to yourself when you get stressed. A little reassurance that everything is going to be A-OK."

My brain actually says the opposite of that. "Nope. Don't have one of those."

"Think about creating one. They can be very helpful. You could say something like, 'I believe in myself,' 'Today is going to be a great day,' or 'You've got this, Goldberg!'"

I like her. She's funny. "Sure. I'll think about it."

Ms. Laffin's eyes narrowed. "And listen, if you're worried about the Switcheroo Dance, you should know you're not the first student to come by and see me about that . . ."

Mission: Abort! Mission: Abort! I'm NOT talking about that stupid Switcheroo Dance right now.

"Oh . . . that's not . . . I don't . . ." Rube shoved his notebook back into his pants.

BRRRRRRRRRING!

Yes! Saved by the end-of-the-day bell.

Ms. Laffin opened her desk drawer, retrieved a sheet of paper, and handed it to Rube. "These are the tools I mentioned. They're very simple things to do when you feel overwhelmed or when those bubbles start bubbling."

"Thanks," Rube replied. He folded the paper into a square without looking at its contents and stuffed it into his pocket.

"Bye!" Rube darted to his locker to grab a few things before meeting up with Boob and Pearl. He was desperately looking forward to hanging out since they hadn't done so in a while. But before that, he had a mission to complete. Rube strapped on his newest contraption and positioned himself at the entrance to the school courtyard. *This way you can't miss me!* Students immediately gathered around, eager to see what the fuss was all about.

"*This is the Distributor!*" Rube exclaimed. "It's a simple way to pass out multiple flyers at the same time. And today I'm using it to

spread the good word about my friend Pearl Williams. A vote for Pearl is a vote for the future! Pick Pearl for sixth-grade class president! She's the best."

Everyone was fascinated by Rube's new contraption. They swarmed him like a pack of wild dogs, pawing at the machine and taking photos of it for their social media. *One at a time, please. I'm not some circus animal here for your amusement!* In a matter of minutes, Rube's flyers were almost completely gone. *One left. Not too shabby.*

Boob snatched the final flyer from Rube's machine. "I'm loving this new look," he said. "It's very *Iron Spider*. Nice zit too. *That*, I don't love so much." *Smart-ass.* Boob craned his neck in every direction, looking for someone. "Guess Zach was too busy to help out, huh?"

"He wasn't at school today," Rube replied. "Must be sick or something."

"Mm-hmm. *Must be*," Boob said, reviewing the flyer thoroughly. "Ick! What's up with the cheap paper quality? These aren't the ones Pearl made."

"I printed these myself," Rube said, proud of his effort. "There's even a special treat on the back. Check it out."

Boob flipped the flyer over.

Nestled at the bottom was a small square filled with the tiniest text. "It's a no-homework pass, like a coupon, that you can give your teacher so you won't be penalized if you didn't do your homework. Genius, right?"

"That's brilliant!" Boob exclaimed. "Pearl doesn't know you did this, does she?"

"Nope. And don't say anything to her either. I want her to be surprised."

"Oh. She'll be surprised, all right. This no-homework pass? It will not end well, my friend. It will not end well."

"Look, if Pearl wants to win, she has to do something big and bold."

"Her *ideas* are big and bold, doofus."

"You don't get it . . ." Rube shut down Boob's dissention as Pearl approached. "Here she comes. Don't say a word. *I mean it*, Boob."

Sometimes telling Boob not to do something made him want to do it even more. This instance was no exception. "Hey, Pearl," he said, trying his best not to break.

"Oooohhh." Pearl was impressed by Rube's wearable machine. "Love the new look, Rube. It's very *Iron Spider*," she said. "What's the occasion?"

"This is the Distributor. It's a machine that passes out multiple flyers at the same time. I'd give you one, but we just ran out."

"You were passing out *my* flyers?" asked Pearl.

"No, I was passing out flyers for Mr. Spicy's Chili Hut," Rube replied. "Yes, I was passing out *your* flyers. The crowds were eating them up!"

"This is awesome, and I love it, but . . . can we *not* talk about the election? It's been stressing me out, and today is my day off from extracurricular activities. I just want to hang out at the Lair and chill. Can we do that?"

Rube saluted. "Aye-aye, Captain." *Anything for you.*

Little did he know that Emilia had been watching everything unfold from her window perch inside the second-floor library, and she was not pleased. "This is a betrayal," she mumbled softly to herself, closing the curtain and rushing away to parts unknown.

Meanwhile, Rube, Boob, and Pearl biked away to their not-so-secret headquarters as quickly as they could. *Life moves fast. No time to waste.* The Lair was their favorite place to hang out, but it had recently become a hazard. The wooden planks that formed its walls were falling apart. Its ceiling was leaky. Toadstools were popping up in curious new places. Rube used to think a couple of coats of paint might spruce the place up, but the Lair was going to need more than that if they wanted it to survive.

"When are we going to fix this place up?" asked Boob. "My baby needs love."

Rube took a seat at the meeting table. "*Soon*, m'boy. *Soon.*"

"Who's up for some chess?" Pearl asked, digging in her backpack. "I brought my fold-up board."

"Heck, no!" exclaimed Boob. "What idiot plays chess with a chess master?! Your skills are unmatched! I'm not about to be embarrassed like that. What we should *really* do is level the playing field and engage in a li'l game of Truth or Dare."

Nope. No way. Not doing that. Cursed game.

Rube got up from the table and pretended to see something in the woods. "Was that a deer? Might be a bear. Better go investigate!" He rushed out of the Lair and into the forest. *Very believable, Goldberg. A brilliant performance. Way to sell the mystery.* Pearl and Boob were onto his tricks, but they followed him outside regardless.

"One of these days we need to build a rope swing," Pearl said. "Or a hot tub! *That* would be amazing."

"I like where you're going with this," Boob replied. "A bubbling cauldron of luxury."

Rube wasn't feeling it. "There's no way. First of all, how would we get a giant hot tub all the way here? Second of all, we'd need an independent power source to make the jets function. Sounds like too much work. Not worth the trouble."

"Hard to believe there's a job too big for Machine Boy," Pearl said. "Thanks for crushing my dreams, Debbie Downer."

I didn't mean . . . ugh . . . what I meant to say was . . .

"Remember when we found that creepy doll?" Boob asked, pointing to a pile of old timber. "Thing smelled like a sewer pipe. All soggy and gross. And it's still out there somewhere, you know. *Watching us.* Waiting for the right time to strike."

After reading a book about local legends, Boob was convinced the creepy doll they'd found in the woods contained the ghostly spirit of a little girl named Gladys. When strange occurrences had started happening at school, rumors swirled that the doll was a cursed item and whoever possessed it was cursed too. Later, it had been revealed that Principal Kim spread the ghostly rumors as a way to get attention for Beechwood Middle School. However, the creepy doll had gone missing and had never been recovered. And though Principal Kim was deeply remorseful over his deception, no one ever found out where the doll had come from in the first place.

Rube put his hand on his friend's shoulder. "We've been through this. You're not cursed. That whole thing was a sham. Trust me, buddy, there's nothing to worry about."

"*Someone* still has that doll," Boob insisted. "Don't you ever wonder who put it here for us to find?"

"No," said Rube. "People throw litter in the woods all the time. Once we found half a boat in the creek, Boob! A creepy doll isn't that big of a deal."

"Zach knows a lot about the woods around here. His dad owns

a bunch of acreage or something. I'll ask him what he thinks next time we hang out," Pearl said. Rube and Boob stared at Pearl suspiciously. "What? We've been going on nature walks and getting to know each other. You two aren't my *only* friends."

Rube glared at Pearl. "You didn't follow the plan. We were supposed to be lying low and staying under the radar, remember?"

"Right. Because you think Atwater is going to kidnap us and throw us in some secret prison? That's insanity," Pearl said with a smirk. "Also, Zach wasn't a part of that agreement. So there."

"Did you bring him to the Lair without us?" Rube asked.

Pearl folded her arms. "Maybe."

"Sounds like you're dating to me," Rube shot back.

Don't do this, Goldberg. You're being rude for no reason. Well, not exactly NO reason, but c'mon, lighten up. You came here to relax with your friends. Don't start unnecessary trouble!

Pearl shook her head. "Just because we've been shopping in town and taking silly photos in the park doesn't mean we're *dating.*"

"Oooohhh, silly photos in the park," Boob said, wiggling his fingers. *"Saucy."*

Rube shrugged. "I'm just sayin' . . ."

"No, you're not. You're trying to start trouble and be difficult. When was the last time y*ou* hung out with Zach, Mr. Give-the-Guy-a-Chance? Oh, and in case you don't remember, all the stuff I've done with *him*, I've also done with *you*," Pearl explained. "Besides, if Zach and I are going to the Switcheroo Dance together, we need to get to know each other. Have *you* even hung out with Emilia at all?"

The dreaded question! I knew it was coming sooner or later. Rube had been avoiding Emilia's calls and texts at all costs. *What am I supposed to say to her? That I don't want to go to the dance anymore?* At school, he had started ducking behind columns in the library and hiding under desks to avoid Emilia. *Not some of my proudest moments.* But the Switcheroo Dance was coming up, and soon he'd have no choice but to face the music. "We've *hung out* at school . . . kind of . . ."

"That sounds like a *no* to me," Pearl said. "Are you going to the dance, Boob? You don't have to be asked, ya know. Just go by yourself. Then you can mingle as much as you want. It'll be fun!"

Boob winced. "I like to dance with my friends, not around *other people*."

"Reina is going by herself . . ."

"Really?!" Boob blurted out. "I mean, of course she is. That's cool."

As the trio wandered through the woods, they came across a curious patch of land where the trees had been cut down and the ground had been dug up. A man-made clearing that recent rainfall had transformed into a muddy pit. There was a sign, located on the outskirts of the clearing, that warned against trespassing. *Ominous.* In the bottom corner of the sign was a logo featuring a thick black circle in a white box. Boob leaned in close to read the fine print.

"The Null Corporation?" he asked. "What's that?"

"Some company that's buying property all over the place," Rube replied. "The town council is letting them do it."

Boob rubbed his chin curiously. "Hmmm. *Kooky.*"

While the boys were busy staring at the sign, Pearl reached

down, grabbed a handful of soft mud, and shaped it into a small projectile. *THWACK!*

What the?! Rube had been hit in the arm by a well-packed mud pie.

"Did *I* do that?" Pearl snickered. "My hand must have slipped."

"Oh, it is *over* for you, Williams . . ." Rube said, scooping up a handful of mud. "Eat it!" He clumsily threw it in her direction, but it failed to make contact.

"Oops. Ya missed! Can't build a machine to save you now, Goldberg."

"Take cover!" Boob shouted.

As Rube picked up his feet to run, his shoe got stuck, causing him to flail and fall backward directly into a puddle of thick brown muck. *PLORSH!* He lay motionless, looking up at the canopy of trees above. *This is actually sort of soothing.* Then a vengeful thought popped into his head. He sat up quickly and began swinging his muddy arms in all directions, splashing Pearl with tiny bits of sludge. *That'll teach ya!* She tried her best to escape, but Rube grabbed her ankle and pulled her into the puddle, laughing as they flicked mud at each other playfully.

"This is nice," Rube said. "But I feel like we're missing something."

"Or *someone,* perhaps?" suggested Pearl.

All eyes were on Boob, cowering behind a stump. "Don't even think about it!" he shrieked. "These are my favorite pants!" *He says that about every pair of pants he owns.*

Pearl and Rube latched on to Boob's leg and pulled him down into the quagmire with them. As the three friends lay there making mud angels and giggling, all of the tension left Rube's body. He was, at last, relaxed. The little stresses that ate him up inside were forgotten, if only for a moment.

"There's mud in my crevices," Boob said. "It's squishy."

Pearl sighed. "Can we stay here forever? Let's just stay here forever."

Yeah. Let's stay here forever.

CHAPTER 10

"There they are! My gals!"

The lunch ladies at Beechwood Middle School were one of a kind. Adored by some, feared by others, celebrated by all. *Plus, their grilled cheese will blow your mind. Three different kinds of cheeses! From foreign lands! Best in the tristate area.* The lunch ladies didn't put up with antics *or* tomfoolery, which was one of the many reasons Rube and Boob loved interacting with them so much. And the feeling was mutual.

"Uh-oh. Here comes *trouble*," Maude said, clocking Rube and Boob's arrival. She was the brains behind the operation. Her recipes and elite cooking skills turned basic dishes into something special. *She's got a spice rack you wouldn't believe.*

"*Double* trouble," Hildegard concurred. She was the brawn, carrying giant steel pots of boiling soup wherever they needed to go. Her strength was unparalleled. Even the coaches were envious.

One time, I saw her lift a crate of milk with one hand. True story.

"Don't listen to them, boys. *I've* got you covered," Armani said with a wink and a smile. She was the beauty. When Armani looked at you, it was as if she could see directly into your soul. *And she always gives you extra helpings of Nachos Grande.*

"What's the latest gossip, Rube?" asked Hildegard. "I heard you really gave it to that trottel, Atwater. Good for you."

"Trottel means *jerk* in German," Boob mumbled.

Maude shook her head. "Atwater won't let me use my special seasoning in the meatloaf anymore. Said it's too expensive. I told him he's full of—"

"*Easy*, Maude," Armani said. "We don't want to get ourselves or the boys in trouble." She scooped heaping helpings of mac 'n' cheese onto Rube's and Boob's trays. "Don't tell anybody, but you two are my favorite students. We're all very proud of you for speaking up."

"Just doing my part," Rube replied.

As the boys moved through the line, they noticed that posters for the Switcheroo Dance were now plastered *everywhere.*

"Have you and Emilia talked yet?" Boob asked. "She's probably mad you haven't. Or sad. Maybe a little of both. You're going to have to face her one of these days."

"*I know that*. Don't you think I know that?"

"No, I don't. 'Cuz you act like she never even asked you. I haven't heard a peep from you about any of it! Do you even want to go with Emilia?"

Rube wasn't interested in answering that question, but his reply escaped his mouth before he could stop it. *"No!" Oops. Didn't mean to say that out loud.*

"What?! Then *why* did you say yes?"

Grrrrrr. "I was being nice! She put me on the spot, and I didn't want to make her feel weird. Stop worrying about *my* date and worry about your own. Oh, wait. You don't have one."

"Hahaha. Touchy, touchy, Mister Goldberg," Boob chuckled.

"I haven't decided if I'm going to the dance, but if I do, I don't need a date. I'm perfectly fine going by myself. *I'm* not the one who's desperate to make someone jealous . . . "

What does that mean?

The boys paid for their lunches and retired to their table to dig into their yogurts, crunch on their carrot sticks, and stuff their faces with Armani's famous chicken salad among other things. But an unexpected surprise was waiting just around the corner. *Like always.*

"Rube!" shouted Emilia.

PFFFFFFFFFT! Surprised by Emilia, Rube spit his chocolate milk across the table.

Speak of the devil.

"Where have you been? We need to discuss our plan for the dance!" Emilia retrieved a notepad from her pocket. "First of all, *outfits.* I'm wearing a chunky gold sweater and a black skirt. Fall feels. Keeping it casual. I need you to wear a suit. Something fitted. *Fashion preferred.* Also, my parents want to have us over for pre-dance cocktails." She stopped herself. "*Mocktails.* Whatever. Oh, and I need to know what your machine does so I can plan my social media around it."

Rube was confused by that last part. "I'm confused by that last part . . ."

"You're making a machine for the dance, right? *Everyone* thinks you're making a machine." Emilia's tone was sour and harsh. "So, what is it?"

"No wiggling out of this *now*, Goldberg," Boob murmured. "You are *sca-rewed*."

Choose your words carefully, Rube. I mean it this time.

"It's a supersecret surprise," Rube said, faking a smile.

Nice one. Now you've got to make something that'll impress the whole school. Again.

Emilia considered the prospect. "That actually works for me! Yay!" As she moved to give Rube an awkward peck on the cheek, Pearl and Reina showed up with news.

"Atwater is here again and—" Pearl was taken aback by Emilia's sudden show of affection. "Oh. Sorry. Did I interrupt?"

"Nope!" Rube said, hastily sliding his chair away from Emilia. "Just finishing up some business." *Please don't ask what business I'm taking about.*

Pearl and Emilia stared icily at each other, unblinking. In recent days, a rash of gossip had spread throughout the school regarding their campaigns. There were rumors, both silly and vicious, spreading like wildfire. Who had started them? The students had a good idea. Emilia liked to play dirty. Pearl didn't. Neither candidate felt like addressing the other at this moment, so Reina stepped in to break the ice.

"Emilia, the accusations your campaign made about Pearl lacking school spirit are gross and unfounded," she said. "I demand you retract them and apologize immediately."

Emilia grimaced. "Don't know what you're talking about."

Reina refused to let up. "Yes, you do. *Don't play games.* Not only have you been spreading rumors, but a trash can full of Pearl's crumpled-up flyers was found near the science lab, and your fingerprints were all over them."

"The Li'l Sleuthy Detective Kit tells no lies," Boob crooned.

"Care to explain?" asked Reina. "Or do we take this matter to the top? I'm sure Principal Kim would have something to say about this gross injustice."

"Ugh, *fine,*" Emilia huffed. "Sorry about the school spirit thing. And yeah, my fingerprints were all over those ugly flyers. So what? Politics is a game, and *I'm* going to win. That's all you need to know." She put her notepad away and patted Rube on the head. "Can't wait to see you all dressed up, handsome. Bye!"

I'm very very VERY uncomfortable right now.

After Emilia left, Pearl turned to Rube and Boob. Bigger things demanded their attention. "Atwater is coming. I'm going to confront him in front of everyone, and I need you to back me up."

"Whoa. Should we be wearing armor?" asked Boob. 'Cuz that

guy looks like he wants to body slam us every time we open our mouths."

"We've got your back. No question," Rube countered. "But are you sure this is a good idea?" He gestured to the hundreds of students in the lunchroom. "Atwater isn't going to like being called out in front of the world." *That's why it needs to happen, doofus.* "Never mind. I answered my own question. Please proceed."

Soon Atwater barreled through the lunchroom like a freight train. He hated being in student spaces with a fiery passion. But his hunger outweighed everything, and there was only one place to buy hot food in the building. Pearl saw him coming and made her move.

"Hello, sir!" she exclaimed, chasing after Atwater. He pretended not to hear. "Excuse me? Superintendent? I'd like to share something important with you." The room fell silent as Atwater kept walking. "I tried making an appointment and going through all the proper channels, but I didn't receive a response . . . " His pace quickened but Pearl wasn't letting up. "I have a petition here, signed by more than four hundred students, teachers, and parents, demanding that the truth about Beechwood's history be taught in school." Atwater stopped, turned, and reviewed the petition. "Took Reina and me a few days to get them all, but I think it's important that people be heard."

"*You* collected these?" he asked.

Pearl nodded. "Reina did too."

"Hi!" Reina said, waving. "We've met before. You probably don't remember because you were in a boiling red rage."

Atwater flipped through the pages of signatures, eyeing each and every one. "Do you think this means some-

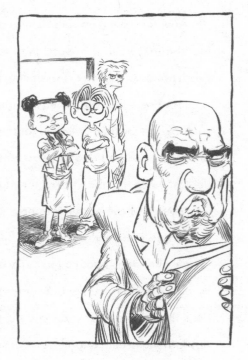

thing?" He ripped the stack of papers in half and tossed the remnants on the ground. "*I* make the rules around here. *You don't*. Be a good little girl and sit down."

Atwater loomed over Pearl in a threatening way. *Not gonna happen, jackass!* Rube swiftly moved in between the two of them. "Pardon me," he said. *Don't even try it*, he meant.

"And what do you think *you're* doing, boy?" the superintendent growled.

Rube didn't hesitate. "The right thing. You've probably never heard of it."

Atwater slowed his roll. He was still seething with anger, but the fact that everyone was watching made him deeply uncomfortable. Pearl, however, couldn't stop smiling.

"It's fine that you ripped up the petition. I made copies," she said. "Some of them went to local news organizations along with other information I dug up. According to my research, Superintendent Atwater, if it hadn't been for your family's money and influence, you wouldn't have gotten into prep school *or* college. I've seen your transcripts, and they're *not pretty*. Before joining the school district a couple of months ago, you actually didn't do much of anything. But I suppose being friends with Senator Wharfman has its perks. Which begs the question: How do you have a job in education without a *background* in education? Don't answer. I'm sure we'll find out soon enough. Anyway, thanks for your time. Enjoy the rest of your day!"

She's unbelievably good. And thorough!

Atwater assessed the situation and realized he was at an impasse. There was no easy way out of this, and any move he made would be the wrong one. *Eat it, Atwater!* He shot Pearl and Rube each a dirty look, then angrily retreated to the front office. As soon as he was out of sight, the lunchroom exploded in rapturous applause. Students were so impressed, they hooted and hollered until they were blue in the face. *Wow. Awesome.* Pearl was completely overwhelmed by the warm reception.

"Whoa," she said, breathless. "For a minute there I wasn't sure that was a good idea. But now I feel like I might actually win this election."

"What did I miss?" Zach asked, arriving on the scene. "Just walked by Atwater in the hallway. He looked like someone peed in his Cheetos."

"I'll tell you later," replied Pearl. "C'mon, Reina. Let's go revise my speech for the student forum. I've got a million new ideas and need to get them out of my brain *now*."

As the girls scurried off, talking about campaign details as they walked, Zach felt annoyed that he'd been snubbed by his future date. "She leaves just as I get here? That's messed up. What's her problem?"

"Pearl is probably looking for Gladys the Creepy Doll," Boob replied. "Know what I'm talking about?" Zach scrunched his nose in confusion. So did Rube. *What is Boob on about now?* "Oh. Sorry. Guess I was thinking of something else. Anyway, how was your day at the park with Pearl, Zach? Heard you two have been hanging out lately, getting hot and heavy."

"We had a blast," Zach said. "Things have worked out really well for Pearl and me since the three of you decided to lie low. More time for us to get to know each other."

As Zach pulled out his phone and flashed a series of photographs from his time with Pearl, an inexplicable feeling came over Rube. It wasn't nervousness. It wasn't anger. He suddenly felt insecure.

Ugh. Insecurity is a bad feeling. BAD FEELING. Not a fan.

"Oops!" Zach cried out. "Some of these pics are not for everyone." He quickly shoved the phone back in his pocket and shot Rube a wink. "Private thing between Pearl and me."

Oh, is it now?

"Pssst. *Hey.*" Boob unzipped his backpack and showed off two cans of soda to Zach. "Smuggled these babies in this morning. You like? Dare me to drink one?"

"Right now?" Zach's eyes glistened with anticipation. "Drinking soda during school hours is a highly illegal activity."

"Bet *you* can't drink one in less than a minute."

Zach couldn't resist the challenge. "Watch me." He reached into Boob's backpack, grabbed a can of soda, and popped the top. "Down the hatch." Rube and Boob watched in awe as Zach gulped down the entire thing in less than thirty seconds. "*BUUURRRRP! What else you got?*" Zach tossed the empty can toward the trash, but Boob caught the thing and stuffed it in his backpack.

"For recycling purposes," he cooed.

Rube was entertained by Boob's newfound affinity for Zach. But he was also suspicious.

Is my best friend playing a game?

And if so, am I a part of it without even knowing?

Rube's heart started to race as his anxiety bubbles began brewing once more.

Hey, where's that paper Ms. Laffin gave me, anyway?

CHAPTER 11

After weeks of flyers, buttons, gift bags, and the occasional dramatic moment, it was Friday afternoon. The election was three short days away. It was now time for the Student Government Forum, the event where every grade's candidates, from secretary to president, made their pitches to Beechwood Middle School about why their classmates should vote for them. *BORING! Usually. But not today.* Today there was electricity in the air. Something felt different this time. Attendance was optional, so expectations were generally low. *Only bookworms and teacher's pets go to school stuff when they don't have to. Or so I thought!*

Rube poked his head into the auditorium and was surprised to find the place packed to the gills. *Standing room only? Boob's knees are gonna hate that.* The room was buzzing with excitement as students settled in to hear the candidates speak. Outside in the hallway, things were much quieter. *And a tinge more stressful.*

"How do I look?" Pearl asked. She was pacing back and forth, wringing her hands nervously. "Scratch that. How I look doesn't matter! It's what I've got to say that matters." She stopped abruptly and peered into the distance as a thought occurred to her. "Should I just throw in the towel? Maybe I should just throw in the towel. Is it too late to throw in the towel?"

Rube and Reina had been watching Pearl talk to herself for the past five minutes, thinking she'd wear herself out and move on. *But she just keeps going.* Rube wasn't used to seeing Pearl stressed out. *She's always so calm, confident, and put together. Seeing her doubt herself is tough. I'm supposed to be the messy one. Yeah, that's right, I said it!* Reina definitely wasn't having any of Pearl's self-defeat.

"Snap out of it!" Reina exclaimed. "You're Pearl Williams, chess champion, honor roll student, baker, daughter, etcetera, etcetera! You're not afraid of this. You're not afraid of *anything.*"

"Snakes. I'm afraid of snakes. And vampires! But they're not real." Pearl gripped Reina's arm in a panic. "Are vampires real?! Do you have any garlic on you? Holy water? Anything?!"

A couple of students were late to the assembly and were thrilled to see Pearl preparing for her big moment outside. "You're so amazing," one of them said. "The way you stood up to Atwater the other day was awesome. He's the worst."

"Good luck in there," said the other. "We're all rooting for you!"

The kind words brought a smile to Pearl's face. "Thanks," she said as the students snuck into the auditorium. "Well, *that* was nice to hear."

Rube offered up a helpful reminder. "You've been hustling harder than any other candidate in any other race. I've never seen someone care as much as you do. You're making a difference! A wise person once said, 'The best view comes after the hardest climb.'"

Pearl rolled her eyes. "He reads a couple books and all of a sudden he's an inspirational quote machine," she joked. "I just wish I knew what Emilia was thinking so I can make sure I say the right thing when she challenges me up there."

"Comparing yourself to your opponent isn't worth it. Each of you is offering a different vision. Focus on *that*," Reina said. "From what I've heard, you've got the best platform of anyone running—and that includes the seventh *and* eighth graders. Apparently once you've been here a year, you give up. And that's good news for you, because you work harder than anybody! Students are excited to elect someone who cares. *And that's you!*"

"I just wish I had more time . . ."

Reina looked her square in the eyes. "Time is a construct," she said with a straight face. "Go in there and do what you came here to do. End of story."

Principal Kim's voice echoed from inside the auditorium. "And now, the candidates for sixth-grade president!"

"That's me." Pearl hugged Reina and opened the door. "Wish me luck."

"Go get 'em, tiger!" Rube exclaimed. "And remember: 'When it comes to justice, there is no easy way to get it. You can't sugarcoat it. You have to take a stand and say, "This is not right." ' "

The words stopped Pearl in her tracks. "Claudette Colvin said that."

"Did she? Huh. I must've read that in a book," Rube said, batting his eyes in a joking way. "Oh, one more thing—when in doubt, make a baseball reference. People eat that stuff up."

"Noted," Pearl said. She went into the auditorium, followed by Rube and Reina, who met Boob, Davin, and Zach inside. The five of them stood against the back wall of the packed space. Pearl continued on down the aisle, entering from the right side of the stage, Emilia from the left. They met in the middle for a cordial handshake before taking their seats.

"Good luck," Pearl said.

"I don't need it," Emilia replied.

Principal Kim quieted the room and introduced the first speaker. "Please give a warm Beechwood Middle School welcome to our first candidate, Emilia Harris."

Students clapped and cheered as Emilia glided to the podium like a pageant winner greeting her fans. She wasn't holding any papers. *Good sign for Pearl, unless Emilia is fabulous at talking off the cuff.* She cleared her throat and dove right in. "I want to begin by giving a shout-out to my girls—Chelsea, Courtney, McKenna, Destiny, Kayla, Gigi, Serena, and Brooke. You're my besties and I love you. Most of the time. LOLZ. Um, so, I didn't prepare a speech because honestly, I didn't need to. My daddy told me to speak from my heart, so that's what I'm going to do . . ."

This should be interesting.

"Like, I want our school to be *good*, but I don't think we need to worry about everything so much! Let the adults do their jobs.

They know what they're doing. It's not like we need to know about school budgets and funding. We have *enough* to worry about, like school, our grades, and saving up to buy a car in five years." Emilia grew distracted by her long pink fingernails. "Meanwhile, my opponent or whatever thinks money grows on trees, which is funny considering she can't even plan a successful garden event . . ."

A round of "boo"s was heard from the back of the room.

"Shut up. You're so stupid," Emilia mumbled under her breath. "The fact is, Beechwood Middle School doesn't need more money. The money we have just needs to be spent the right way. I was thinking we should do a Winter Bash with a snow machine where we all wear white. Like, you can't get in *unless* you're wearing white. Oh, and maybe in the fall there should be a hayride. Other schools do stuff like that and it's fun, so why can't we?" Pockets of spontaneous clapping broke out in the crowd, pleasing Emilia. "My brother has a band—they're actually really good—and we can hire them to play. I'd also like to talk about the *disgusting* food at this school. I don't know where those lunch ladies came from, but they're bad at their jobs and need to be fired."

Okay, you do NOT talk about my gals like that . . .

"I propose that lunches be catered daily by my uncle's catering business. He can give us a really good deal on tacos, which is why I'm also proposing an extension of Taco Tuesday to Wednesday and Thursday, along with the addition of a brand-new state-of-the-art quesadilla bar." The crowd went wild. They hollered so loudly, Principal Kim had to use his bullhorn to quiet them down. "Plus, I will work hard to have not *one* but *two* new soda machines installed by Christmas. After everything we've been through lately, I think we deserve them. And we also deserve a new paint job, 'cuz this place is ugly. In closing, vote for me because I'll do all the things you want. Thanks!"

"*WOOO-HOOOOOO!*" Emilia stood at the podium, soaking up all the cheers and accolades reverberating around the room. The crowd's positive reception was everything she'd hoped for and more. *Just you wait.* She nodded at Pearl and sat down, delighted with her performance.

"Please give an equally warm Beechwood Middle School welcome to candidate Pearl Williams," Principal Kim said. A solid round of applause carried Pearl to the podium, where she placed her speech in front of her, took a long, deep breath, and looked out at the student body. They were anxiously awaiting her response, and with Superintendent Atwater nowhere in sight, she was ready to speak her truth.

"Thank you so much, Principal Kim." *You've got this, girl.* "I love Beechwood. And I love this school. But the truth is, we're not at our best. We *could be,* but the people in charge of this school district have taken money meant for our education and used it for themselves. Lala Palooza generously donated a large sum of money to our school, but where has that money gone? No one can tell me. I ask you to look outside at our superintendent's shiny new sports car, then ask your-

selves, do *you* have everything *you need* to succeed? New books? Clean gym clothes? Look at the walls, where the paint is peeling. Look at the broken lights that flicker. Look at your surroundings and ask yourselves, *Is this how it's supposed to be?*"

"Who cares?!" a voice shouted. A wave of giggles vibrated through the crowd.

Pearl giggled too, but not for the same reason. She was entertained, having expected this kind of response. Pearl was more than prepared to tackle a heckler. "*I care. Students* care. *Teachers* care. *Parents* care. And you should care too. This isn't elementary school; this is the *big leagues*. You want people to take you seriously and not think of you as children? Then *step up to the plate!*"

Two baseball references?! NICE.

"We don't have to be kids. We can be young adults. But we're going to have to put the work in. We can make our school and our town better by telling the truth, learning from past mistakes, and building stronger systems. I believe in this school, and I want us to have the best things we can. Like programs and textbooks that teach the full scope of American history, a thriving STEM program, and yeah, maybe a quesadilla bar too, among many other things. Join me in starting a movement to change this school for the better. A vote for Pearl Williams is a vote for the future!"

The crowd went ballistic, and Pearl ate it right up.

"And no homework!" cried a boy in the front row. He was waving one of Pearl's flyers in the air. "Homework sucks!"

"What did you just say?" Pearl asked, befuddled.

This is not good.

Students all over the auditorium began waving Pearl's flyers, chanting "No homework! No homework!"

A girl ran up to the stage and handed Pearl a flyer. She eyed it suspiciously. "It looks like mine, but the paper quality is terrible and . . ." She flipped it over. "A no-homework pass?! Who did this?!"

As one, everyone turned toward the back of the room and pointed their fingers at none other than Rube Goldberg.

"Told ya," Boob whispered in Rube's ear.

Pearl struggled to find the right words as the crowd grew restless. "Even if I win the election, homework isn't something *I* can control."

"You lied to us!" a boy shouted. "Liar!"

Then the booing began. As the crowd became unruly, Pearl stood at the podium, tears welling in her eyes. Her grand speech had been ruined, and one of her best friends was partially to blame. Emilia tried not to grin, but she couldn't help herself. Overwhelmed, Pearl grabbed her speech and ran out of the auditorium as Rube followed behind.

"Let me explain—"

"What universe do you live in, thinking that a no-homework coupon is a *good* idea?! Are you kidding me, Rube?!" Pearl exclaimed. "I can't make that happen! I'm not a sorceress!"

"I'm sorry . . ."

Pearl scoffed. "Yeah, yeah, yeah. You're always *sorry*. Anytime you do something without thinking, you're sorry, which is, by my count, *all the time*. It's becoming really tiring."

Zach burst out of the auditorium, brushing Rube aside in the process. "Don't think about *him* right now," he said, comforting Pearl. "You did great up there. That's all that matters." Zach turned to Rube, staring daggers in his direction. "Can you give us a little space right now?"

The nerve of this guy!

But Rube did what he'd been asked to do. *Step aside, Goldberg. You messed up.* There was no sense in arguing about it. *Pearl was right; I do act without thinking. It's becoming tiring for me too.*

After school, Rube went home and stuffed his face with cheesy chips and drank himself silly. *On lemonade.* He needed to talk to someone who'd listen, someone who'd sympathize but remind him to keep his eye on the prize. But no one was around.

Grandma Etta was out. Boob was at his brother's wife's cousin's baby shower. Zach was obviously a no-go. With Bertha unable to communicate outside of barks and farts, Rube was stuck talking to himself.

Unless . . .

He whipped out his phone and dialed up Lala. *Let's hope she's game for a video chat.* Lala hadn't been in school much lately, preferring to be tutored at home. *She tends to disappear like that. Money allows her to get away with stuff other people would get in trouble for.* Surprisingly, she answered on the first ring. "Hey! Whatcha doin'?" asked Rube.

"Contemplating my place in in the universe," Lala said. She was splayed out in her luxurious bedroom, lounging comfortably with her cat, Rolex. "What's up? Did someone get suspended for doing something shameful? Was one of our teacher caught on camera mooning someone at a football game? Tell me something scandalous!"

"No scandals here. Not really. It's been a while since you were at school, and I just wanted to talk. What gives? Is everything all right?"

"School is just *so boring*. My private tutor has been bringing me my work. It's so much easier than waking up every morning and pretending I want to be there."

"Must be nice." Bertha leapt up on Rube's lap for a snuggle. "Lala, do you think I need a mantra?"

"Absolutely."

DING, DING!

Lala received an alert. "OMG, Ami Patel just texted me. Did you give out no-homework passes and say they were from Pearl?! Because apparently *everyone* is talking about it right now."

Gah! Are you serious?!

"She says Pearl and Zach were at the Inside Scoop after school and people were giving them a ton of heinous looks. What did you *do* to that poor girl, Goldberg?! You're going to ruin her chances of leading our school to greatness!"

"Don't yell at me! I didn't do anything! I was just trying to help!" Bertha didn't like it when Rube got upset. She rolled around next to him, nuzzling his body, trying to get his attention any way she could. *Yes, I see you, girl. Kinda busy at the moment.*

"Did you truly think you were helping? Because *I* would've thought that silly scheme through just a teensy bit more. For a smart kid, you make some dumb decisions sometimes." *She's got me there. I really need to work on that.* "Did you talk this through with your little sweetheart Emilia?" Lala's voice dripped with sarcasm. "It would be *juicy* if you did."

"Emilia and I don't really talk that much, actually. Or hang out. She sent me a reminder text about what I should wear to the dance, but I haven't responded."

"I'll never understand why you said yes to her." *Because she asked me.* "And don't even think about saying 'because she asked me.' That's! Not! A! Good! Reason! Emilia is bad news. Her dad tried to kick my dad out of the country club they both belong to. That family is trash."

"Rich people problems," Rube said, rolling his eyes. Suddenly, an idea blasted into his brain like a rocket. "Emilia thinks I'm debuting a machine at the dance tomorrow night, but what if I made a machine for Pearl instead? There's gotta be a problem she needs solved."

"You should definitely make a big exciting machine everyone will talk about for weeks! But please, *for the love of god*, lose the Pearl angle. Haven't you put her through enough already?" Lala sighed. "I hate to say it, but you're toxic right now, Rube. At least as far as Pearl is concerned. Accept that for the moment and move on." *Like a dagger right through my heart.* "When she wants to talk to you again, she'll talk. In the meantime, you and I need to have a chat about something *else*." *Great. What did I do now?!* "My birthday is coming up, and I'm thinking about having a party."

Phew. That was a close one. "Cool! I'll bring chips."

"You better bring more than that. Remember how I went out of my way to help you pull off your big stunt after Con-Con crashed and burned? Well, I've been thinking, and I've got a few ideas for how you can pay me back."

Before Lala had a chance to pitch her ideas, Rolex spotted Bertha on Rube's lap and lunged at the screen like a beast. *"RAOWRL!"*

"Stop it, you psychopath!" Lala screeched as the cat clawed the screen. "I have to go, Rube. Rolex is being a monster. Listen, don't stress! Talk soon. And remember—nous triompherons. Nous prévaudrons. Ensemble!"[1]

Wait. What did she just say?!

---

1 French translation: "We will triumph. We will prevail. Together!"

But Lala was already gone.

Rube looked into the eyes of his trusty sidekick. "We need to learn French, don't we, Bertha?" He sat there for a moment, playing on his phone, searching random things online. *Omelets. How much are sneakers? Spider-Man Miles Morales. How do you make chocolate cake? Where to buy chocolate cake online? Junk sales in Beechwood. Who is Professor Butts?* Rube wasn't sure what he was looking for, but he didn't find any new information on any of the subjects he searched. *Oh well.*

He put his phone away and strolled to the kitchen to make himself a snack, but upon seeing his antique toaster sitting proudly on the counter, an idea began to form. "Change in plans," he said, rubbing his hands together. "Time to get to work!"

CHAPTER 12

The wait is over.

The Switcheroo Dance was either going to be the event of the season *or* a sparkling embarrassment of epic proportions. *We're about to find out!* After his chat with Lala, Rube's mind drifted to all kinds of places as he got to work on his machine. At the front of his brain was Pearl. *In the past few weeks, I've made so many preventable mistakes that it's like I'm unknowingly sabotaging our friendship. Is that even possible?* Rube desperately wanted to make it up to Pearl in a big public way. Thankfully, this time his brain advised him against that. *Lala's right—I need to leave Pearl out of it.*

What he did instead was build something fun. Just for himself. *If I have to go to the dance, at least now I'll be able to enjoy it.* He spent the whole day Saturday tinkering with his creation while Bertha played in the backyard, but as the hours passed, Rube's nerves crept in with a vengeance. *For so many reasons.* He was nervous about meeting Emilia's parents. *Even though we're not a couple.* He was nervous about seeing Pearl. *We're not a couple either.* And, strangely, he was nervous about dancing in front of the whole school. *Stupid, I know. But I have a plan to combat that.* As for the other stuff, all he could do was hope everything worked out.

Once his machine was finished, Rube hopped in the shower, put on his suit, and dabbed himself with a hint of his dad's fancy cologne. *Just a hint, don't worry.* After hiding his surprise machine in the locker room at school for easy access—*the custodian leaves the side door unlocked!*—he raced to his Emilia's house to meet her family and take photographs.

Unsurprisingly, Rube showed up drenched in sweat and out of breath. He had also missed "mocktail hour." *But hey, I look good!* Rube was dressed in a vintage suit his mom had bought him at a flea market when he was little. At the time, it had been way too big for his small frame, but now it fit like a glove. *A very tight glove.* All he knew was that he hadn't followed Emilia's outfit suggestion. *If this isn't fashion, that's not my problem. I think I look good!* Would she be upset? *We're about to find out.*

DING-DONG!

The door opened and Rube was met with an unexpected yet familiar surprise. He was welcomed into the house by the town council person who'd harassed the Rosens at the Treasury. A man who just happened to be *Emilia's dad.*

"You must be Rube," he said, giving the boy a once-over. "I'm Mr. Harris. Huh, have we met before? You look very familiar."

And so begins a new round of anxiety bubbles.

"I just have one of those faces," Rube said, grinning like a fool.

He's gonna hurt me, isn't he? I'm gonna end up cut into pieces and dumped in a river.

Mr. Harris eyeballed Rube with laser focus. "No. I've *definitely* seen you before."

Welp. The jig is up. I'm going down. Tell Bertha I love her. Goodbye, cruel world!

"You're the machine kid! I read about you online."

Oh! Well. My, my, my. It seems my reputation precedes me.

"I am!" Rube said in an extra-chipper voice. *To throw him off my scent.* "The machine kid from online! Have a problem that needs solving? I'll make you a machine for it! Hahahaha!"

Relax, Goldberg. Now you're acting like a loon.

Before Rube embarrassed himself further, Emilia descended the stairs dressed in the exact outfit she had told him she was going to wear. *Predictable.* Her reaction to Rube's ensemble was less than favorable, leaning toward panicked. "That's *not* what I told you to wear."

"I *did* get your text. But I liked this suit better. It's vintage! I think it once belonged to a criminal because there's a peculiar red stain on the inside of the jacket pocket. Might be blood."

Emilia glared, unblinking. "Let's pretend you didn't just say that."

Mr. Harris ushered the unhappy couple outside (*we are not a couple!*), where Mrs. Harris snapped photos and gushed over how good her daughter looked before rushing away to teach one of her famous online yoga classes. Mr. Harris, who would rather have been sitting in his favorite chair watching TV, drove Emilia and Rube to the dance. The car ride was awkward and silent. *For the most part.*

"Does your dad like being on the town council?" asked Rube in a hushed tone.

"I guess," Emilia scoffed. "Why do *you* care?"

"Just asking." *Way to make things even more awkward than they already are.* Rube's nerves started to fray as the car pulled up to the school. *Keep it together, Goldberg. You're already here, so try to enjoy yourself. Don't mess things up for a change.*

"Is the machine all set up?" asked Emilia. She pulled out a small makeup mirror and did one last mug check. "I want to take photos with it as soon as we walk in."

"I'm not unveiling it until later. Don't you want to mingle first?"

Now Emilia was steamed. *"No."* She swung open the car door, almost hitting Pearl and Zach as they walked by. "Sorry. My bad." *There's no plane of existence where that girl is ever sorry for her actions.* Rube nodded at Pearl. Pearl nodded at Rube. Zach grabbed Pearl's hand and pretended they were closer than they actually were.

Two can play that game. Rube grabbed Emilia's hand, but she flung it away in disgust. *"Don't." All righty then, looks like tonight is going to be a real blast.*

"Time to party!" Boob shouted. He burst onto the scene dressed in a tuxedo T-shirt and sequin pajama pants, movin' and groovin' down the sidewalk like he'd just won the lottery. *The guy has a style all his own. Can't help but love him.* Since his parents owned a fabric store, Boob had access to all kinds of exotic textiles. *And this is what he chose.* "Who else is feelin' like a million bucks? And, yes, to answer your question, *I know I look good.* Who said a guy can't go to a dance alone and have a good time?!"

"No one said that," Rube replied. "We *all* said you should go to the dance alone *because* you'd have a good time."

"And I listened," said Boob.

Just then, Reina rolled in. *On her bike.* The metal music from her headphones was loud enough for everyone to hear. "Lookin' good, Boob," she said, riding into the courtyard. "Didn't think you were gonna make it. What an interesting *sequin of events.*"

"Hehe," Boob replied. "You look good too, BTW."

"Went with a throwback look from one of my favorite old movies," Reina said, locking up her bike. "C'mon, let's go dance!"

Boob was slightly hesitant. "Uhhh, this isn't a date, *right?*"

Reina rolled her eyes and sighed. "No. *This is not a date.* We're

just two randos walking into a dance together. Jeez, kid. Loosen up a little, wouldja?" She grabbed Boob's hand. "I've got your back. Don't worry." She pulled him inside as the rest of the crew followed closely behind.

Here we are. Our first formal event as middle schoolers. A rite of passage! Doesn't look as tacky as I thought it would. That's a good sign.

The gym had been done up with all the typical decorations. There were streamers, balloons, and Switcheroo Dance signs. *Basic but tolerable.* The theme was unclear, so the planning committee had hung a bunch of Beechwood Bandicoot flags everywhere. *For that extra touch of school spirit.* Supposedly a band was going to play, but the gym's stage remained dark. Principal Kim had stuffed some old computer equipment behind its curtain, making it a less-than-desirable performance space. In one corner of the room, local DJ Tommy T was spinning all the latest hits. In another corner sat the refreshments table, surrounded by faculty chaperones standing guard. As more students arrived, the dance floor got busier, but there still weren't enough people out there for Rube's liking. *If I'm gonna shake my butt, it has to happen in a large crowd. Those are the rules.*

While Emilia was busy gabbing with her friends, Rube scooted away to the punch bowl, where Rube's algebra teacher, Ms. Shankar, kept a vigilant watch.

"Well, well, well. Is that *John Travolta* I see?" she asked. Rube started to blush. "Looks like someone's got some *Saturday Night Fever*! Are you ready to *boogie-oogie-oogie*?"

I don't know what any of those words mean.

"I just saw Principal Kim doing the Dougie," Rube said. "He's a decade late, but you have to give the guy credit for putting in *some* kind of effort. Why aren't you on the dance floor, Ms. Shankar? Two left feet?"

"Ha! No. I'm actually trained in jazz, hip-hop, and modern dance," she explained. "But someone has to guard the snack tray. Can I interest you in a celery stalk slathered in ranch dressing? Or perhaps a very soggy, hypoallergenic peanut butter alternative and jelly square?" Rube turned up his nose. "Yeah, me neither. But they were all we could afford."

You better get your head in the game, Goldberg. Tonight's the night you wow the crowd with a machine that will revolutionize dancing! As Rube thought about his big surprise machine, excitement turned to worry as he imagined what horrors might befall him. *What if someone finds my machine and sabotages it? I heard Mike and Ike were planning some rotten prank. They're not smart enough to execute one smoothly, but what if tonight is the night they raise their game?* He downed a cup of cheap fruit punch and slammed it on the table. *Ahhhh. Good stuff.*

Rube scanned the crowd for Pearl and Zach but couldn't find them. *They're probably making out in the corner. Or taking cheeky photos with the Beechwood Bandicoot. I hope they're happy together with their three kids and two-car garage. Pffft. I gave those two the best years of my life!* Creating whole fictions inside his head was kind of new for Rube. Obsessing over things that were both *out of his control* and *none of his business* was not. That kind of thinking made him sick. He downed another cup of fruit punch, then reached into his pocket and pulled out the list of tools Ms. Laffin had given him. *Maybe it's time I did something about this yucky feeling.* Then his stomach did a fartwheel. *Too much cheap fruit punch. Gettin' some thunder down under. Better head to the boys' room.*

On the other side of the gym, Boob was decidedly less active, sitting by himself in the bleachers. After walking into the dance with Reina, he had quietly slipped away when she wasn't looking. There was too much stimulus for him to manage, and his nerves had gotten the best of him. Reina was disappointed to have lost her partner in crime and went looking for Boob, searching the shadowy areas of the gym for traces of his presence. He evaded her at every turn. But now her keen loner senses had locked on to his location. He was finally out in the open, and there would be no escape.

"Help me understand something," Reina said, stomping up the bleachers toward Boob. "You got all dressed up in sequin pants and *don't want to dance?* You must realize that doesn't make any sense. How can you possibly look *this* good, listen to *this* music, and *not* want to shake your booty?!"

"It's not that I *don't* want to dance, it's that I don't want to dance *here* in front of the entire school," Boob said, shifting in his seat uncomfortably. "I'll just draw attention to myself. And *I know* it's a stupid excuse. But that's how I feel right now."

Reina sensed there was something much deeper going on. "Sequin pants attract attention. We both know that," she said, sitting down next to Boob. "But if there's anything else you want to talk about, I'm here to listen."

Boob hung his head low. He wanted to tell Reina every thought inside his noggin, but there was so much to say that he was afraid once he started talking, he might never stop. "What made you choose the name Reina?"

"It means 'queen' in Spanish. I almost went with Lily, since that's my favorite flower. But, for the record, Velma from Scooby-Doo is my style inspiration. Those glasses, that hairstyle. *Big* fan."

"Velma is an *icon*. Her intellect, her humor. We have no choice but to stan. I've been trying *desperately* to get Rube and Pearl to form a mystery-solving gang with me, but so far, it's just me. They think I have a crush on you, by the way."

"*Hmmm.* Are you *sure* they think that?"

Boob turned away, pretending not to hear. "Were you afraid when you came to school different from before?"

"Not really. I feel *less* afraid now. Of everything. For a long time, I wasn't true to who I was, but now I'm finally myself. And I love it! I feel *free*, ya know? Like I don't have to hide who I am."

Boob bit his lip like he was about to burst. "I have to tell you something . . ." He wrung his hands a few times and then let loose. "I like boys."

Reina smiled. "Cool. Me too. Even though they can be super annoying."

Boob smiled. "Guilty as charged." He ran his fingers

through his hair nervously. "You're the first human I've told."

"First . . . human?"

"My stuffed animals know. I told them a while ago. But we're not currently talking. It's a long story. Furby knows what he did."

"So, do you feel better now? Like a weight has lifted?"

"I feel good. *Weird.*" Boob began bopping his head to the music. "But *good.*"

"Hehe. You're finding your groove, I see. Why haven't you told your friends?"

Boob winced. "I'm scared. I know I shouldn't be. They're the best. But what if they think I lied to them all this time and never talk to me again? That's my worst nightmare!"

Reina put her arm around Boob and pulled him close. "Your friends love you. *A lot.* They want you to be happy, dummy. I do too. You're *beautiful*, my friend. And not just because of those incredible sequin pants."

Boob chuckled to himself. "No one has ever called me beautiful before. Now I feel weird, good, *and* uncomfortable. Score!"

"Welcome to life, Boob," Reina replied. "Do you like breakfast sandwiches?"

"Only a demon from the depths of the netherworld would deny the deliciousness of a fresh sausage, egg, and cheese."

"Biscuit, roll, croissant, or bread?"

"If I make it? Bread. If my mom makes it? Biscuit. One day when I live in New York City? Roll. If a fancy French chef is in my kitchen? Croissant."

"We're in agreement on all counts! But enough about that." Reina grabbed Boob's hand and yanked. "C'mon. We're dancing."

"*Wait.* I have another confession to make," Boob warned. "I've never actually danced in public before. The only place I dance is in my room by myself or with Rube. People watching me dance makes me feel uncomfortable. My limbs are long. I look like a wild noodle! *And* I get really sweaty. Also, sometimes I dance like I've got poison ivy on the bottoms of my feet. I can't explain it. Just . . . don't make me do this. *Please.*"

"I totally respect your point of view and everything, but honestly, nobody cares about any of that but *you*," Reina said. "What's the worst that'll happen?"

All of a sudden, there was a spot of trouble on the horizon. Mike and Ike were moving through the crowd, headed in Boob and Reina's direction. Rumors swirled earlier in the week that the twins were looking for revenge on Reina after the embarrassing incident at the Inside Scoop. What better place to enact it than here, where everyone would be gathered, for maximum embarrassment? At school the twins had kept a low profile, but now, even among the mass of students, those two ogres stuck out like a couple of ginormous sore thumbs.

As they got closer, Boob spotted them and rushed to protect Reina. "Get behind me," he said. "I'll deal with these numbskulls."

But something was off about the twins. The closer they got, the more it looked as if they were upset.

"We just wanted to say . . ." Mike sniffed. His eyes welled with tears. "We're sorry." Ike nodded silently in agreement. Their expressions were sullen and somber. Mike wiped his runny nose on his sleeve. "That's all." Mike and Ike had been carrying unknown burdens on their shoulders, and it was clear Reina's words at the Inside Scoop had touched a nerve. It wasn't clear what hardships the twins had endured in private that had led to such a rare outpouring of emotion, but, it didn't matter. Two of Beechwood Middle School's biggest jerks were acting like human beings for the first time *ever*, and that was enough to celebrate.

"Cool," Reina said. "Apology accepted." The music blared, and having mended fences, there was only one thing left to do. "Wanna dance?" The twins looked at each other, then back at Reina.

"Yeah," Ike said softly. "Th-th-that would be nice, actually."

"Whoa, whoa, whoa!" Boob squealed, waving his hands in the air like a referee. Getting serious, he turned to Reina and spoke in a hushed voice. "Are you *sure* you want to do this?"

"They came over here to make peace and they deserve a second chance," Reina replied. "Besides, *you* won't dance with me!"

Boob reconsidered. "Good point. Now that there's peace throughout the kingdom, let us *all* DANCE and BE MERRY!" he shouted. And with that, the quartet made its way to the dance floor to begin an interesting new chapter.

Meanwhile, on the other side of the room, Rube's stomach had become a knotted ball of frustration. *What else is new?* In a bold proclamation, loud enough for everyone to hear, Emilia had decided she didn't want to dance. *No reason given.* Instead, she pulled out her phone and affixed herself to the wall. *Oh! So that's where the term* wallflower *comes from. I didn't get it until just now. Small world!* Rube pulled up a chair and sat down next to Emilia to keep her company, but she was more interested in checking her social media. *As per usual.* Her eyes may have been fixed on her phone, but her body language indicated that she was hungry for Rube's attention. His eyes were elsewhere.

"If you're going to reveal your big machine, you need to do it soon," Emilia said, trying her best to be nonchalant and failing miserably. "My hair is looking really good right now. *Ugh, it's so hot in here.* Can you please just go get your machine now? I told my followers I'd post a pic! It's getting really late and . . ." Emilia noticed Rube was looking at something in the distance and followed his gaze to its destination. "Are you staring at Pearl?!" she screeched.

Suddenly, Rube was jolted from his trance. *Yeah, I guess I am staring at Pearl.* She was on the opposite side of the room, sitting alone, and had been that way for quite a while. *She doesn't seem upset.* On the outside she looked fairly content, but Pearl was good at hiding her emotions when she wanted to. Emilia poked Rube, demanding an answer.

"Excuse me. *I'm talking to you.*"

"*Yes.* I'm staring at Pearl." *Obviously.*

"You're here with *me.*"

"And yet your phone is getting all the attention . . ."

Emilia didn't like hearing that. "*Excuse me,* who do you think you're talking to?! My followers expect me to deliver content. I planned on doing that *tonight,* but so far you haven't come through." *She asked me to the dance because she wanted to use me for my machines. My first groupie! How exciting.* "And don't think I'm ignoring how you completely ghosted me these past few weeks. If you didn't want to come here with me, you should have just said *no.*"

She's right. She's absolutely right. I lied to Emilia when I should have told her the truth. In a nice way, of course. No need to be cruel. A lie of omission is still a lie. But I didn't speak up, and now here we are. "You're absolutely right. Sorry about that."

"OMG, you're admitting it?! You didn't want to go with me this whole time, just stringing me along like a simp?! *Wow.* This was a bigger mistake than I thought."

"*You bet it was.* Honestly, at first, I was flattered by the attention you gave me. It felt nice. Even though you were *way* too intense about it. I'm truly sorry that I didn't speak up. I need to do that more often. But being nice to me and asking me to the dance just so you can get a snap of my machine? That's embarrassing. I'm embarrassed for you. So, I'm going to go now."

Rube was feeling himself like never before. The truth, as they say, had set him free. And he couldn't contain his newfound independence. He got up from his chair, shook his legs out, and did the Electric Slide onto the dance floor, leaving Emilia in the dust.

Now, that's more like it.

Rube needed some face time with Pearl. *Immediately.* He spotted her near the outskirts of the conga line, danced over to her, and tried his best not to be annoying. "I haven't seen you with your date since you got here," Rube said.

"He bailed as soon as we walked in."

"BOO. That stinks. Funny, though, since I'm learning that Zach can be kind of a . . ." *Cut the gossip, Goldberg. Tell her what you did. Tell her your surprise! It'll cheer her up.* "Oh. Hey. Forgot to tell you. So, um, I signed up to be a poll worker on election day."

"Really? You know you have to get there *before* school starts, right?"

"Yep. I already made a machine that has four different alarms just in case," Rube explained. "Figured it was my duty to support the democratic process! Who knows, maybe next year I'll run for office." *Now, there's a thought.*

FWOOSH!

Suddenly, the music stopped, the doors to the gym flew open, and a team of burly security guards flooded into the space. Lala Palooza had finally arrived. No matter how many classes she skipped, Lala would rather die than miss an important social engagement. She was dressed in an extravagant outfit, which she happily posed in as a handful of student photographers surrounded her. The dance floor cleared immediately to make way for her grand entrance.

"You don't have to do that," she announced for all to hear. "I know I'm flawless, but I'm not royalty." Everyone had their eyes on Lala, but Lala's eyes were searching for someone else. "Aha. There she is." Her target spotted, Lala rushed over to DJ Tommy T and handed him an MP3 player. "I curated this playlist myself. It's got a much better vibe. *No offense.* Oh, and I'll double whatever the school is paying you. For your trouble." DJ Tommy T plugged in the device and cranked up the beats. "Okay, everyone! Back on the dance floor!" Lala demanded.

As the students returned to their positions, Lala made her way over to Pearl, cozying up next to her. "Got your text. Zach officially sucks. But we knew that, right? Forget these boys. We have bigger things to think about, girl. Our options are, number one: getting the heck out of here, or number two: staying and showing these goons how to party. What'll it be?" Lala noticed Rube hovering close by and gave him the stink eye. "Don't *you* have somewhere to be, Goldberg?"

Oops. Oh yeah. I guess it's time for the big reveal.

"BRB!" Rube said, slipping away to the locker room, where his latest creation was waiting undisturbed. *There it is. So sweet, so delicate. Look at you, my prize!* The centerpiece of his dancing machine was his new antique electric toaster. *The perfect addition! At the perfect time.* The wearable contraption required Rube to strap himself in like an astronaut heading to space. *Not an easy task to accomplish by yourself, but I can do it!* After some comical struggling, he adjusted the cumbersome apparatus and checked himself out in the mirror. *Not bad, Goldberg. But one of these days I've got to work on my leg muscles. Gotta get swole! Oof, this thing is unwieldy.*

Slowly and carefully, Rube ambled down the hallway, making sure not to bump the machine into anything that might break it. *This is it. Your grand return to greatness! Buckle up, Beechwood. Here comes the next big thing.* Fifteen minutes after leaving, he opened the door to the gym and slowly made his way back inside, wearing the outfit to end all outfits.

"Hear ye, hear ye! Bask in the glory of the Hoofer!"

Everyone stopped what they were doing and turned in his direction.

"School dances can be difficult when everyone wants to cut a rug with *you*. But worry no more, booty-shakers! The Hoofer allows its wearer (me) to change dance partners seamlessly! And now for a demonstration. Hit it, DJ Tommy T!" The lights got lower. The music got softer. Lala's playlist had been replaced by the dreaded *first slow dance of the season*. Rube waddled over to Pearl and Lala, the Hoofer weighing heavily on his body. "Would you ladies like to d—"

Before he could finish, the Hoofer's immense heft caused Rube to lean to one side, then the other. Soon he was doing a quirky two-step movement as he tried to regain his balance, moving in circles around the dance floor like a Spirograph. *Whoa, I can't control this thing!*

Davin, trendsetter that he was, spotted Rube shuffling around the dance floor and saw an opportunity to get the crowd excited. "Do the Rube!" he shouted, mimicking Rube's movements. DJ Tommy T switched up the music and soon everyone, *teachers included*, were doing "the Rube." It was awesome!

However, Rube himself was still trying to find stability. "One sec," he said, his voice shaking. "I've almost got it." Pearl and Lala cringed as he made a final attempt to get a handle on the burdensome device. Then the inevitable happened. *Aw, nuts.* The weight of the Hoofer was too much for Rube to bear. *I've lost control.* He toppled to the ground with a *THUD*, breaking the machine into pieces.

My precious toaster baby, apple of my eye, item of power, char-er of breads for more than one hundred years. Gone in the blink of an eye. Grrrrr. This really sucks butt!

In an instant, Rube and his machine had become a joke. *A laughingstock, to be honest.* As students jeered around him, all Rube could do was lie on the ground in a daze. *Maybe I'll just stay here forever.*

Then an odd thing in the corner of the gym caught his eye. Professor Butts, dressed in his trench coat, was watching the commotion from the shadows. *What the—?! The Professor, here?! That can't be. Somebody must have spiked the punch.* He did a double take, but the Professor was still lurking. As people gathered around Rube, his view of the Professor became obstructed. "Move! Get out of the way, please! I'm trying to see something!" He batted at people's legs like a maniac, but by the time they cleared out, the Professor had disappeared. *Not on my watch.*

Rube unbuckled himself from his contraption and slithered through the crowd on his hands and knees. *You're not getting away that easily, Butts.* He busted open the doors to the hallway and caught the Professor fleeing at the other end. "Save me a dance!" Rube shouted back at Pearl. "I'll be right back!" He took off down the hall, running as fast as he could after the speedy Professor. It didn't make sense that an old man like the Professor had such a spring in his step, but Rube tried not to think about it too much. *Maybe he drank some cRaZy jUiCe or something?*

After rounding a handful of corners, Rube tracked his quarry to the area behind the stage, where it was pitch-black. The lights were hard to find in the dark, but Rube knew just where they were. *Here we go.* "I've got you now!"

He flipped the lights on to find a shocking sight! Zach was assembling a machine of his own.

"This isn't what it looks like," Zach warned. "I-I-I . . ."

"Where's the Professor?!" cried Rube.

Zach's jaw dropped. He wasn't sure what Rube was talking about. "The Professor . . . ?" he muttered in confusion.

Without a second of warning, Boob burst through the curtain, sweaty and out of breath. "I knew it!" he shouted. "*I knew it, I knew it, I knew it!* Oh, you are *goin' down*, Zachy-boy." He reached into his pocket and pulled out a slip of paper. "Allow me to introduce Exhibit A—a fingerprint I lifted from the soda can you touched the other day. Now, you may ask yourself, why would I want your fingerprint? Funny you should ask!" He pulled out a second slip of paper. "So, I could compare it to *this*! Exhibit B—a fingerprint I lifted from the antique toaster Rube received in the mail recently. He thought his dad had sent it to him, but I had a sneaking suspicion he hadn't, so I lifted the print just in case, and *guess what, bucko?* It matches your print from the soda can."

Rube was baffled by what was happening. "What's going on here, Boob? I don't understand . . ."

"To be honest, I don't either," Boob said. "But it's definitely something fishy, and thanks to my Li'l Sleuthy Detective Kit, I'm

the one to uncover it. *There's more.*" He pulled out yet another slip of paper. "This right here is the first fingerprint I ever lifted. Ahhh, *memories.* Want to know where *it* was from?"

"Yes!" Rube shouted. "Of course I do!! You just waltzed in here and dropped some major mystery junk on me! Why would I *not* want to know what that's from?!"

"Jeez. You don't have to yell," Boob said, waving the slip of paper through the air to taunt Zach. "*This* fingerprint was lifted from Gladys the Creepy Doll before she went missing. You'll never guess who it belongs to . . ."

Zach lunged toward Boob, grabbing at the slip of paper. "Give me that!"

Rube stepped up, blocking his path before he made contact. "You better have a good explanation for this, *friend,*" he said, his eyes narrow and focused.

It was time for Zach to come clean and he knew it. "Boob is right." Zach's voice was soft and defeated as he confessed his sins to Rube. "I followed you to the Lair and tossed that doll in the woods nearby, so you'd find it. Then I stole it back, so you'd think something sinister was happening at school. Then, when you told me your dad was in Phoenix, I found that antique toaster online and had it sent to you from there so you'd think it was from him."

Rube was more than a little bewildered. "But . . . I still don't . . . understand . . ."

Zach gritted his teeth as he grew angry and frustrated. "*You* don't understand?! Ha! Join the club, genius. *Neither do I.* I'm just following orders." He flipped a switch on his machine, and it began to purr. "All I wanted to do was make new friends and live a normal life, but *he* wouldn't let me." Zach grabbed hold of the curtain rope. *Uh-oh.* "For what it's worth, Rube, I'm sorry. Maybe someday we'll both understand." Zach yanked on the rope, opening the curtain and revealing a strange machine to everyone in attendance. *What the heck is this thing supposed to do?*

The assembled students stopped dancing and turned their undivided attention toward the stage, where the machine turned on. In an instant, a gigantic poster unfurled in front of everyone. Printed on the poster was a photograph of Pearl, in the park, laughing and picking her nose. *OMG, this is bad.* A clump of snot sat at the end of her finger. *OMG, this is really bad.* Below the image was the campaign slogan, PICK PEARL, in green gooey letters.

OMG, this is really really bad!

Having accomplished his strange and damaging mission, Zach ran out through the back door in a flash, leaving Rube and Boob on the stage by themselves, frozen like two frightened raccoons caught stealing trash from a garbage can. *Nothing makes sense.* Rube's heartbeat quickened. He started hyperventilating. Every eye in the auditorium was fixed directly on him. *Anxiety bubbles? More like anxiety boulders, crashing around inside me, breaking into pieces and tearing up my insides until there's nothing left but shredded organs. This is the worst feeling ever.* Rube's nervousness intensified when he looked out into the crowd. There was Pearl, stone-faced, in shock and disbelief. Before he had a chance to speak, the fire alarm sounded.

WEEEEOOOO! WEEEEOOOO! WEEEEOOOO!

Next came the rain . . .

FSSSSSSSSSSSSS!

There were many things that needed fixing at Beechwood Middle School, but the sprinkler system was still in excellent shape. *Thankfully. But in this case? Not so much.* As a deluge of water discharged throughout the entire building, there was total mayhem. Students ran for cover as teachers ushered them out of the auditorium. People slipped. People tripped. No one was safe from the flood of chaos. In his haste to take control of the situation, Principal Kim knocked over the refreshments table, spilling red punch all over his new suit. The Switcheroo Dance and all its attendees were completely and utterly drenched. Rube and Boob stood on the stage, calmly watching the anarchy unfold. Rube fished Ms. Laffin's list of tools out of his pocket, but the sprinklers quickly turned it into a soggy paper napkin. *So much for that.* Rube balled it up and tossed it over his shoulder.

What a mess. What. A. Mess.

CHAPTER 13

Beechwood Middle School smelled musty.

A different kind of musty than usual.

After Saturday night's surprise shower, the entirety of the school had been professionally cleaned so it would be nice and fresh for Monday morning when the students returned. Hiring a team to complete such a task on short notice had cost the school district an arm and a leg. *There goes more of that STEM money.* But the job had gotten done. *Even though it still kind of stank.* Sadly, many things throughout the school were completely unsalvageable. Soaked classrooms meant soaked lesson plans, books, and supplies. On Sunday, the teaching staff had jumped into action, pooling their money and buying new materials so everything would be good to go on Monday. Some things were simply irreplaceable. However, hope was on the horizon.

Though Rube and Boob were initially suspects in what came to be known as the *Switcheroo Sprinkle*, an abundance of evidence

swiftly cleared their names. Security cameras had caught all of Zach's misdeeds. *The setup, the execution. It was all there.* On his way out of the building, Zach had pulled the fire alarm, but not before lighting a handkerchief on fire and waving it under the sprinklers so they'd detect the heat and activate. *He thought of everything.* But Zach's ruinous actions had consequences, and over the weekend he'd been kicked out of school. Principal Kim had warned the faculty not to speak of it, but rumors and whispers were plentiful. *Aren't they always?*

Rube wasn't sure what to think or who to believe. When Zach had been caught red-handed, he copped to sowing all kinds of chaos. *But why? Why did he do all of that? Nothing makes sense.* The worst part of the brouhaha was that Pearl and Rube still hadn't spoken. She knew all about Zach's betrayal thanks to a flurry of texts from Boob and Lala. *But she still won't talk to me.* Rube tried not to think about it. He had other important matters rattling around in his brainspace. *I have poll-working duties to fulfill!*

When Monday morning rolled around, he got up at the crack of dawn, ate a healthy breakfast, and was waiting in front of the school when the custodian unlocked the door. *The early bird gets the worm!* Poll worker rules stated that no one could show support for their candidate of choice, so Rube removed his official PEARL HAS A PLAN pin and put it in his pocket so he wouldn't get in trouble.

"Let's get this show on the road . . ."

After setting up the check-in table and voting booths, Rube waited patiently as students lined up outside. But waiting patiently had never been Rube's strong suit. *You should know that by now.* So his mind wandered to machines—more specifically, to a simple, hands-free way to place each ballot into its respective box. *The Justice Deliverer!* But after so many recent missteps, Rube put a pin in his new idea to focus on what was in front of him. Today was all about Pearl, and with so much riding on her success, there was no room for distractions.

"Move it or lose it! Hot breakfast sammies comin' through!" Boob arrived for moral support with a sack of yumminess in his hand. He plunked down next to Rube and pushed a warm sausage, egg, and cheese sandwich in his direction. "Get egg-cited!"

Sniff, sniff. "These don't smell like the ones you get from Toasty's."

"They're not. Reina and I made them this morning. Big days require homemade treats! Have a bite. I only put a few anchovies on yours." *I think he's kidding. He better be kidding. Aw, who cares? A second breakfast is a second breakfast.* Rube bit into the sandwich and was transported to another planet. "Heaven. I'm in *heaven.*"

Boob noticed Rube was doodling in his notebook. "Whatcha workin' on? A little comic strip? Make me a character! Ya know, the Magnificent Boob has a nice ring to it."

"Nope," Rube said, closing his notebook and putting it away from prying eyes. "The *Annoying* Boob sounds about right, though."

"Watch what you say to the guy who just brought you a tasty treat," Boob replied. "So what's the tea, buddy? How ya holdin' up?"

"Pearl isn't talking to me," Rube said, his mouth full of gooey, eggy goodness. "I know I messed up big-time, but *I* wasn't the one who blew up a giant photo of her picking her nose . . ."

"No, you just screwed up the garden event and passed out fake no-homework passes, which almost got her *kicked out of the election.*"

"Point taken. But what can I do to make it up to her?"

"Well, you'll have to consult a wiser oracle than me on this one. With as many strikes as *you've* got, I have no idea." Boob bit into his sandwich. "I still can't believe your intuition told you that something fishy was going on backstage, so you randomly ran back there and found Zach! Good call." *Yes. My intuition. I definitely didn't chase an old man in a trench coat, who then disappeared mysteriously, through the school.* "What if you're actually developing *mutant powers?* Let's make a rule that you *cannot* be an X-person without me." *Ugh, I really dislike not telling Boob the whole truth, but he can't know about Professor Butts. Not yet. Not until I have a chance to figure out what's going on.* "Did you see Zach's locker was cleaned out? We're not supposed to talk about it apparently."

"His phone number is dead too."

"I hope he's okay. Honestly, I feel kind of bad for that kid."

Rube rolled his eyes. "Yeah, *right.*"

"No, *I do.* What he did at the dance? *Big yikes.* HUGE. Unforgivable. But the way Zach was talking makes me think he's in real trouble. Has it occurred to you that he never let us see his house or meet his family? What if he's got a bad home life?"

"That *still* doesn't explain why he did what he did."

"True." Boob looked at Rube with concern in his eyes, but

neither of them had time to explore the matter further. The student council election was about to begin, and Rube had a job to do. "Time for me to hit the road," Boob said. And that he did.

The voting line snaked around the school from the science labs all the way to the locker room. *That's a good sign.* As Rube began ushering people inside, Emilia's mean-girl squad pushed to the front, her father following close behind.

"I want to see that ballot box, Goldberg," demanded Mr. Harris.

"Never!" Rube shouted, springing into action. *What do I do? What do I do? What do I do? Wait! I know. He can't open the box without the key!* Rube raced over and lifted up the ballot box. *There you are.* The key to the lock was taped underneath it. "This is for democracy!" Rube placed the key under his tongue and gulped, pretending to swallow it.

"What's wrong with you?!" snapped Mr. Harris. "All I want to do is take a photograph of the ballot box for Emilia's social media. I'm not planning on *stealing it.*"

Oh. "I guess that's fine, then . . ." Rube removed the key from under his tongue and placed it back under the ballot box. "Thought I swallowed it, huh? Another classic Goldberg fake-out," he said, licking his lips to remove the foul taste of brass from his mouth.

"Such a strange boy," Mr. Harris muttered to himself as he took his photos and left. After the rush of early voters, the line thinned out quickly. *No time to waste. I run a very tight ship!* A few more of Emilia's friends popped by at the same time as Reina, pushing to get to the voting booth before the first bell rang. Reina wasn't having their rudeness.

"*Excuse me.* You dropped something," she said. The gaggle of aggressive young ladies stopped what they were doing and frantically began searching the surrounding area for lost items, though there were none to be found. Reina's ruse got her to the voting booth before them, where she proudly cast her vote for Pearl. *"Wait for it . . ."*

BRRRRRRRING!

Emilia's friends had officially missed the first voting window.

"Sorry, ladies. Try again later!" Rube exclaimed. "Better get to class now. You don't want to be late."

Feeling defeated, the clique grumbled to one another as they shuffled away.

"You play dirty," Rube said. "I like it."

Reina laughed. "Nothing dirty about that. If they had their eyes on the prize, they might've made it in time. Besides, they'll be back if they *really* care. And if they'd tried to start some real trouble, I would've kicked the cricketbutter out of them anyway."

"You've been spending time with Boob, I see," said Rube. "Be warned, once you start using his weird lingo, he'll never stop trying it out on you."

"Haha. It's cute. Just like him," Reina replied. "Anyway, I'm out. See you later!"

Cute, huh? Well, isn't this an interesting turn of events?

Everyone went their separate ways except Rube, who was left by himself to wait for his replacement. Sixth graders always worked the first shift. Mid-morning was for seventh, and lunchtime was for eighth. If you missed any of those voting windows, you were out of luck. Rube doodled to kill time until an unexpected visitor showed up.

"Oh," Pearl said, popping her head into the room. "I didn't think you'd still be here."

Rube froze. His anxiety bubbles were doing their thing again. But Rube decided to show them who was boss. *Remember your tools.* Despite his initial reluctance, he'd retrieved the waterlogged list and committed it to memory. *Sometimes making the effort isn't so bad.* He closed his eyes and took two deep breaths. *Think of something calming.* A warm feeling grew in Rube's chest as the thought of his mom's smile glowed brightly in his mind. *Now use your new mantra.*

"You've got this, Goldberg!" he cheered.

Pearl was confused by the outburst. "Uhhh, what?"

"Oh, nothing. Just my new mantra. Anyway, what I wanted to say is . . ." The words came to Rube a lot more easily than he expected. "Sometimes I act without thinking. Which is *kind of* funny, considering how much I think about stuff."

"So funny. *Hysterical,* even," Pearl said sarcastically.

"My brain and my body don't always sync up. But I'm going to work on that. And I promise to do better."

"You should," Pearl said, pleased as punch. She looked around the room at the makeshift voting booths and ballot box and became sentimental. "I couldn't have made it this far without your help, Rube. And when I say *help*, I don't mean those messed-up flyers or your machines. Knowing you have my back means a lot. You can be *really messy*, Rube. But I'm grateful for your friendship."

That feels nice. Now, quick, change the subject before you say something stupid.

"Nice turnout so far this morning! Reina had to muscle past some of Emilia's goons, but other than that, I've got a good feeling about the election. Big things are afoot!"

"*Just so you know*, that was *fake* snot in the photo." *Oh. She's backtracking . . .* "It was slime Zach bought from a gift shop in town. We were just playing around. I don't understand why he did what he did." *No one does.* "And now that he's gone, I'll never get any answers." Pearl sighed. "My brother said kids are talking about what happened at the dance over at the high school, so I've got *that* going for me . . ."

Rube grabbed Pearl by the shoulders and looked her in the eyes. "You are freaking amazing! And I-I-I . . ." Unable to find the right words, Rube let his actions speak for him, putting his arms around Pearl and hugging her tight. *It feels nice to squeeze my friend.*

TAP-TAP! Before Pearl could properly respond to Rube's outpouring of emotion, there was a knock on the door frame. Huxley Wright, the seventh-grade class clown, was there to relieve Rube of his duties. "Physical touching!" he screeched upon seeing Rube and Pearl in an embrace. "Make it go away!" He dramatically covered his face, stumbling into the room, knocking over a coatrack and a stack of chairs. "My eyes are bleeding! I've gone blind from this gratuitous public display of affection!"

"Grow up, Hux," Rube groaned. He and Pearl grabbed their backpacks and headed to class. Before they said their goodbyes, Rube offered one last bit of encouragement.

"You've *got* this."

By the end of lunchtime, voting was officially over and the tabulation had begun. It was a very serious process overseen by a council of teachers and students. By the end of eighth period, the count was complete. Each winner's name was sealed in an envelope and put into a lockbox for safekeeping. In the past, the results had been read over the school intercom. But Principal Kim, in his infinite wisdom, decided such an important event was worthy of an assembly, so three boisterous grades packed into the gym like sardines. *Pure misery for all involved.* For some reason, the order of announcements had been switched at the last minute. Eighth grade was up first, seventh grade was second, followed by sixth.

By the end of the convocation, the students were restless. There was only one council position left to call—sixth-grade class president. *This is it. The moment we've all been waiting for.* Superintendent Atwater hovered over Principal Kim, who held the final envelope in one hand and a microphone in the other. *It all comes down to this.*

"A little breathing room, please," Principal Kim said, shooing Atwater away. He bit his lip and opened the envelope. "The new sixth-grade class president is . . ."

Say it. SAY IT.

"Pearl Williams!"

Cheers erupted throughout the gym! Students danced and high-fived.

Rube's heart swelled for his friend. *She did it! Just like I knew she would!*

But the celebration was short-lived. Atwater swiped the paper from Principal Kim's hand, pushed him aside, and made a move for the podium. "What do you think you're doing?" Principal Kim demanded. He swiped the paper right back and held it just out of the superintendent's reach. "The results are *final.*"

Atwater, however, was undeterred. "There was a *problem* with the voting tabulations. The count was incorrect, and thus *Emilia Harris* is the new sixth-grade president," he growled into the microphone. "And *that* is final!"

The students were puzzled by the strange development. No one knew what to believe. Murmurs echoed through the room as Beechwood Middle School became ground zero for a strange

new mystery. *Something devious is afoot.* Ms. Shankar stormed up to the podium, yanked the paper out of Principal Kim's hand, and showed it to the crowd. The truth was clear. *Pearl* was the next sixth-grade class president. "You should be ashamed of yourself, Superintendent Atwater. The voting tabulations were done in accordance with the rules, and to say otherwise is . . . is . . ." Ms. Shankar was steamed. "Undemocratic! You are completely out of line. And rude! You're also *rude.* You're a rude person. *So there.*"

"Tell him, Ms. Shankar!" a girl cried out.

Atwater was incensed. The veins on his forehead bulged. *Like he's about to change into a werewolf or something.* "This school is *done,*" he snarled. Atwater stormed away angrily, but before he reached the door, Mike and Ike discreetly opened two bottles of hotel shampoo onto the floor in front of him. *Please don't ask me why they had two bottles of hotel shampoo in the first place.* Atwater didn't notice the slick of lightly shimmering goo. *Can you guess what happens next?* He stomped through the shiny puddle and lost his balance, slipping and sliding all over the place. *Major Shaggy from* Scooby-Doo *vibes.* He comically fumbled over and over again, trying desperately to regain his composure but ultimately doing the splits. *Ouch. Looks painful.* The back of Atwater's pants ripped open in the process, sending the crowd into a tailspin of hysterical laughter.

Principal Kim saw Atwater struggling and barely stifled a

giggle. He motioned to Miss Mary for assistance. "Can you . . . ?" She helped Atwater up and walked him out of the auditorium as gently as possible. When the boisterous crowd died down, Principal Kim returned to the podium, regained control, and tried his best to cover for Atwater's bizarre behavior. "The superintendent's tummy wasn't feeling so good, which I think turned him into a little angry-pants. But let's not worry about that for the time being." Principal Kim looked pleased but nervous. He knew he'd have to answer for his resistance at some point, but now it was time to celebrate. "Today I could not be prouder of Beechwood Middle School. We had the highest voter turnout of any election *ever*, and I'm excited to work with our student government to *get things done*." He nervously wiped his suit sleeve across his soggy forehead. "Let's give a round of applause to *all* of our newly elected office holders!"

After the cheers died down and students were dismissed, Principal Kim waved Pearl over so she could view the election results. "See? You won," he said, showing her the slip of paper with her name on it. *"In a landslide."*

There it was in plain sight. *The truth.* Verified by multiple non-partisan sources. Rube, Boob, and Reina joined Pearl to inspect the verified results.

"We're so proud of you, Pearl," said Ms. Shankar. "Your hard work paid off! You did it. Just like we knew you would. If the teachers here still gambled, I would've bet all my money on you without question!"

"You had this in the bag from day one. I felt a vibe," Reina said. "Even Goldberg's never-ending bumbling couldn't mess this up."

Uh, thanks. I think?

Boob had pressing questions for Principal Kim. "Are you going to tell us what was up with Atwater, or are we supposed to make up rumors and spread them around school ourselves?"

Principal Kim furrowed his brow. Despite his closeness with the students, he was still the person in charge. That meant he couldn't speak as freely as he liked. Coupled with the fact that he was now on thin ice with Atwater, one wrong word could end his career at Beechwood Middle. "Mr. McNutt, I know you have questions and I assure you, you're not the only one. All I ask is that you not spread unfounded rumors. For the good of the school. Do you understand where I'm coming from?"

"He does," Pearl said. "But that doesn't mean we're going to stop fighting."

Principal Kim's brow relaxed. "I expect nothing less." A sly grin emerged. "Oh, and we'll be switching out our old textbooks for something newer and more"—he chose his words carefully—"truthful. Your push for change was quite convincing. To me, anyway.

There's still a little finessing to do, but good things are on the horizon. A *new switcheroo*, if you will!"

Pearl shook her head in disbelief. "A couple of days ago, it looked like my whole campaign was tanked. Now we're making real progress! I wonder what changed?"

"Students realized you stood for something important. *That's* what mattered the most to them," replied Principal Kim. "This moment is the beginning of change here at Beechwood, and *that's* something to celebrate."

"Hey," Emilia said, approaching the gathering with caution. *Please be nice, please be nice, please be nice.* "Pearl, I know you might not believe me, but I'm really happy for you." Her voice had suddenly lost its high-pitched twang. *She's actually being real.* "You deserve this way more than I do." Emilia sighed as if a great stress had been lifted. "Honestly, I only ran because my dad pushed me. I won't get into it but *ugh,* he can be the worst." *Ain't that the truth.* "You deserve this. Way more than I do. Start some trouble, girl."

"*Good* trouble, as congressman and civil rights leader John Lewis said!" Principal Kim piped up. "Please. My heart can't take any other kind."

Pearl extended her hand, Emilia shook it, and the tension of the past few weeks evaporated quickly. *Crazy how that happens.*

But there were lingering questions, now more than ever. Good things and weird things were afoot at Beachwood Middle School. *So, we're just not going to talk about Professor Butts's mysterious disappearance?* No, we're not. *Sigh. Fine.*

With the school day at an end, Rube, Boob, Pearl, and Reina strolled over to the bike rack and contemplated their next move.

"I knew this was going to be a good day when I saw two odd-shaped cheese pieces in my snack pack at lunch that looked like those ancient Chinese symbols, yin and yang," Boob said. "It was like the universe was trying to tell me something."

"Yeah," said Reina. *"You eat too much cheese."*

Pearl was ready to hit the road. "Can we celebrate now? I'm thinking a stop by the cupcake shop, then we head to the Lair for some face-stuffing?"

"I'd love to celebrate, but I gotta bolt," Reina said, fastening her helmet to her head and hopping onto her bike. "Great work, everybody. Can't wait to see what happens next!"

"But wait!" Boob screeched. "Where are you going?"

Reina smiled. "Anywhere I want."

Boob waved goodbye like a maniac as Reina rode away into the distance. "She's like a Wild West sheriff," he said, glowing. "She rolled into town, helped take out the trash, and now she's off to parts unknown. A mystery woman of the frontier! It's a good thing she's on our side."

"That's exactly what I think," Rube said.

"Great minds think alike," replied Boob.

Rube had an idea. "What if we celebrated by going over to the Treasury and helping the Rosens go through their storage sheds?"

Boob rolled his eyes. "That's not celebrating! Celebrating is drinking milkshakes until your stomach grows to the size of a basketball, then having *another milkshake.* You're trying to trick us into doing some shady machine business."

"*Actually*, I'm not." *Tell the whole truth.* "Okay, *yes*, I'm always on the lookout for cool machine parts, and *yes,* I'm always thinking about building stuff. But today it's not about that. Today it's about helping the Rosens look for cool antiques they can sell to raise money and hopefully save their business. No shady stuff, only *helping.*"

Boob turned to Pearl. "You're the star of the day. It's up to you . . ."

Pearl stroked her chin in thought. "While I do agree that milkshakes would be nice, I'm always up for doing good instead," she said. "But only if afterward we can buy giant tins of popcorn, lie on beanbag chairs, and watch movies until our bodies become one with the beans."

"Awesome. There are a lot of important things that need doing around here." Rube smiled. "And I'm ready to help get them done."

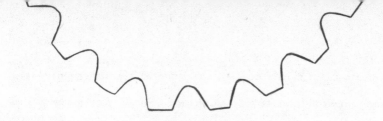

EPILOGUE

On the outskirts of Beechwood sat North Hill, a fancy neighborhood that overlooked town, where the houses had gates and were protected by cameras. The whole area was surrounded by trees, shrouding it in a canopy of mystery. Rube and his friends rarely went there. *It's too snooty*, they'd say. But one among their group had been living in North Hill, right under their noses.

Zach crept through his father's mansion carefully, taking soft steps so he wouldn't make any noise. Though his father hadn't been home in weeks, Zach never knew when he might show up unexpectedly, so he was always careful to complete his chores. Anything less would be deemed unacceptable. On this particular night, all Zach had to do was drop off Gladys, the creepy doll, in his father's study and go to bed. A simple enough task.

But as Zach got closer to the study, he noticed a light coming from underneath the door. His father was home. *This was not good.* Thinking he could get away with a quick and stealthy drop-off, Zach slowly opened the door to his father's quarters, praying it wouldn't creak. No such luck.

"Did you think I wouldn't find out?"

A figure sat in the darkness, nestled comfortably in an old castle chair, facing away from the door and toward a roaring fire. Zach felt his heart drop. It wasn't supposed to be like *this*.

"I did everything you told me to do, Father—"

"And you still failed," the man in the chair grumbled. "Now the Goldberg boy has suspicions, his little gal pal has suspicions, even their *idiot friend* has suspicions."

"But they don't know the whole story. How could they? You're so close to achieving your goals already. By the time they figure it all out—"

"Failure is unacceptable!" The man slammed his fist onto the nearby end table.

Zach trembled with fear, his natural response to his father's heartbreaking cruelty. "It won't happen again, Father. If you're planning on punishing me for my incompetence—"

"Stop blubbering! For bungling my long-term plans for this town, you deserve much more than just punishment. And to think I assumed you might be able to execute this mission. *Tsk, tsk, tsk.* How *embarrassing*. Not only are you a disappointment to our bloodline, you're without value as a human being. Worthless in every way." The man stood up from his throne and moved closer to the fire. "Bring me the toy."

Zack's feet wouldn't move. He was frozen with fear. The man walked over, ripped the creepy doll out of Zach's hands, and violently tossed it into the fire. As the stuffed idol crackled and burned, the flames grew brighter, revealing the identity of Zach's mysterious father: *Professor Zeero.*

"What now?" Zach asked.

"Failure or not, the end is near. So we go underground as the pieces fall into place. The final part of my plan is on the horizon, and no one, certainly not a group of ignorant *children*, can stop what's coming next." A wicked grin sprouted on Professor Zeero's face. "Beechwood is mine."

ACKNOWLEDGMENTS

As always, Jennifer George is our resident guru for all things Rube. She's a supportive and encouraging partner who is never afraid to tell you exactly what she's thinking. Jennifer knows all the right places to slip in Rubisms and add special touches that connect our hero to his real-life counterpart. The same can be said of the great Ed Steckley, whose illustrations capture the magic of Rube's machines while adding his own special touches. Ed brings vibrancy and life to our cast of characters. How does he do it?! We may never know.

Russ Busse was our ship's first editorial captain. He helped get the Rube series off the ground and I'm forever grateful for his input and direction. Then Francoise Bui came on board to provide a new perspective in the interim before Paul Ruditis arrived to steer us into the next chapter. Nicole Overton made some solid suggestions along the way while Margo Winton Parodi, Alison Cherry, and Regina Castillo kept my grammar, punctuation, and syntax in check. Each of these individuals have offered valuable commentary and candid advice, all of which have made this series better.

Hannah Otero, thank you for sharing your family's story with me. It helped ground this book and I appreciate it so much.

Stephanie Laffin, you are a superb sounding board! Enjoy the homage. Travis Kramer, this one's for you! Terry and Jean Snider, I love you to the moon and wouldn't be the person I am today without the love and support you gave me.

I'm grateful to have a community of creator friends who've supported the Rube Goldberg series in one way or another. Preeti Chhibber, Ian Carlos Crawford, Susan Eisenberg, Steve Foxe, Jordan Gershowitz, Merrill Hagan, Jon Paul Higgins, Karama Horne, Gabe Hudson, Frederick Joseph, Randall Lotowycz, Yehudi Mercado, Scoot McMahon, Aaron Reese, Carrie Seim, Dave Scheidt, Christopher Taylor, and Stephanie Williams to name a few. Also, a big thank-you to the Gaffigan family, especially Michael, Patrick, and Katie, who shared their love of Rube with the world.

Thank you to the team at Abrams, including Andrew Smith, Charlie Kochman, Anne Heltzel, Jessica Gotz, Megan Carlson, Deena Fleming, Brenda Angelilli, Chelsea Hunter, Borana Greku, Gaby Paez, Hallie Patterson, Jenny Choy, Kim Lauber, Casey Ward, Jody Mosley, Angelica Busanet, Erum Khan, and Melanie Chang. Additional thank-yous to Laura Nolan, Jill Smith, Bob Bookman, Deb Calagna, Kristen Kelley, and Michael Bourret.

Much love, respect, and gratitude to the librarians, teachers, educators, and booksellers who've supported Rube's journey! We can't do this without you.

ABOUT THE AUTHOR

Brandon T. Snider is the bestselling author of the award-winning *Dark Knight Manual*, as well as *Marvel's Avengers: Infinity War: The Cosmic Quest* series. Additionally, he's written books featuring Cartoon Network favorites like *Adventure Time* and *Regular Show*, and for pop culture icons such as Marvel's Spider-Man and Black Panther, Justice League, Star Wars, and the Muppets. Brandon lives in New York City.

ABOUT THE ILLUSTRATOR

Ed Steckley is an award-winning print and advertising illustrator. He grew up in Racine, Wisconsin, and currently lives in Queens, New York.

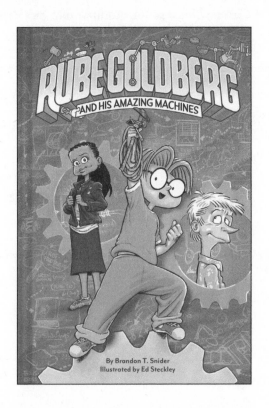